"Shall we get this over with?"

One eyebrow rose in silent query. "Wham, bam—thank you, ma'am?" Dimitri taunted silkily as he moved slowly toward her.

His raking scrutiny was daunting as he lifted both hands and framed her face.

Leanne gave a silent groan of despair as liquid warmth began coursing through her veins....

HELEN BIANCHIN was born in New Zealand and traveled to Australia before marrying her Italian-born husband. After three years they moved, returned to New Zealand with their daughter, had two sons then resettled in Australia. Encouraged by friends to recount anecdotes of her years as a tobacco share farmer's wife living in an Italian community, Helen began setting words on paper and her first novel was published in 1975. An animal lover, she says her terrier and Persian cat regard her study as as much theirs as hers!

HELEN BIANCHIN

Dangerous Alliance

Harlequin Books

TORONTO • NEW YORK • LONDON
AMSTERDAM • PARIS • SYDNEY • HAMBURG
STOCKHOLM • ATHENS • TOKYO • MILAN
MADRID • WARSAW • BUDAPEST • AUCKLAND

ISBN 0-373-11741-8

DANGEROUS ALLIANCE

Copyright © 1994 by Helen Bianchin.

First North American Publication 1995.

CHAPTER ONE

THERE was a soft thud as the Boeing's wheels hit the tarmac, followed by a shrill scream of brakes as the powerful jet decelerated down the runway.

The flight had been smooth and uneventful, and merely one in a series of many which Leanne had taken between the Gold Coast and Melbourne during the past five years.

With one exception. This time Paige wouldn't be waiting to meet her, and there would be no joyous reunion and exchanged laughter as mother and daughter attempted to catch up with each other's news.

An ache began behind her eyes, and she blinked quickly in an effort to dispel the threat of tears as she gazed sightlessly out of the window.

It wasn't fair that her beautiful mother should fall prey to a rare form of cancer, or that its stealthy invasion had proven to be so extensive that the medical professionals could only issue a grim prognosis. Within twenty-four hours of receiving the news, Leanne had arranged her flight and assigned a senior assistant to manage her beauty therapy clinic.

The engines wound down to a muted whine as the large jet wheeled off the runway, then cruised slowly towards its allotted bay.

Customary procedure completed, Leanne joined the queue of passengers vacating the aircraft, unaware of the appreciative glances cast in her direction. Vivid blue trousers and matching top in uncrushable silk accented her slim curves and were a perfect foil for her shoulder-length ash-blonde hair.

Within minutes she emerged into the arrival lounge, and she moved with ease towards the luggage carousel, her eyes skimming the conveyor belt for a familiar bag.

'Leanne.'

The sound of that faintly accented drawl tore the breath from her throat, and her heartbeat stilled imperceptibly, then kicked in at an accelerated rate. It took only seconds to compose her features before she turned slowly to face the man standing within touching distance.

His tall, broad frame was sheathed in impeccable suiting, and strong, sculptured facial features, piercing grey eyes and dark well-groomed hair completed an arresting composite that few women could successfully ignore.

As head of the vast Kostakidas empire, he emanated a dramatic sense of power that was coveted by his contemporaries and viewed with supreme caution by those who chose to oppose him.

Dangerous, compelling, and intensely ruthless. Lethal, she added silently as she summoned a smile in greeting.

'Dimitri.'

Five years ago she would have flung herself into his arms, accepted the teasingly affectionate brush of his lips against her cheek, and laughingly indulged in a harmless game of flirtatious pretence.

Now she stood quietly, her eyes clear and unwavering, their blue depths masking pain. 'I thought you'd still be in Perth.'

One eyebrow rose slightly, and his expression assumed an edge of cynicism in silent reproof. 'Like you, I rearranged my business affairs and caught the first available flight east.'

Her features were a carefully composed mask that hid a host of emotions. 'It wasn't necessary for you to meet me.'

He didn't say anything. He had no need. She was Paige's daughter and his late father's silver-haired angel. As such, he would accord her every consideration, and refuse to concede her desire for independence.

Leanne felt her body quiver slightly, and she forced herself to maintain rigid control. 'Have you seen Paige? How is she?'

His eyes held hers for a few timeless seconds, then his features softened. 'An hour ago,' he revealed. 'She is as comfortable as it is possible for her to be.'

Paige had earned Dimitri's affection ten years ago when she'd married his widowed father, and her warmth and generous nature had turned Yanis's house into a home, softened the hard edges of a cynical, world-weary man whose sole focus in life appeared to be escalating his empire to monumental proportions while grooming his only son to follow in his footsteps. The ensuing five years had resulted in an abundance of love and harmony, until tragedy had struck with a boating accident that robbed them of husband, father and stepfather, and placed Dimitri at the helm of the vast Kostakidas corporation.

'Which bag is yours?'

Dimitri had been educated in a number of countries, and his faint accent was an indistinguishable inflexion that lent itself easily to a fluency in several languages; Leanne shivered faintly as she attempted to maintain a mental distance from an intrusive memory.

'The tan,' she acknowledged, indicating its position on the carousel, and she watched as he extricated it with ease.

'Shall we go?'

It was crazy to feel so incredibly vulnerable, she chastised herself silently as she walked at his side to the sleek, top-of-the-range maroon-coloured Jaguar parked at the kerbside immediately adjacent to the entrance.

Within minutes Dimitri urged the powerful vehicle into the flow of traffic exiting the terminal, and Leanne directed her attention to the scene beyond the windscreen, feeling strangely loath to indulge in idle conversation.

The car's air-conditioning provided relief from the midsummer heat, and the sun's glare was diffused by tinted windows through which the sky appeared as a clear azure, with only a whisper of soft cloud evident on the horizon.

Nothing appeared to have changed, Leanne mused as the Jaguar picked up speed on the freeway. Weathered brick homes dulled by pollution and age-lined suburban streets, and narrow steel tracks embedded into main arterial roads provided a linking tracery for electric trams as they whirred noisily to and from the city.

She drew a deep breath, then released it slowly. Melbourne was a large, bustling metropolis of multinationals with a culture that was wide and varied. It was the place where she was born, where she'd grown up and attended shool.

There was an intrinsic desire to turn back the clock. Except that that was impossible, for you could never recapture the past, she reflected sadly.

Now she'd stay for as long as Paige needed her, and afterwards she'd return to the Gold Coast where, thanks to Yanis's generosity, she owned her own apartment and a successful beauty therapy clinic, ensuring not only financial independence, but a safety net that would enable her to sever the one remaining link to the Kostakidas family.

'No attempt at polite conversation, Leanne?'

His voice held musing humour, and she cast him a pensive glance.

'Your success in the business arena is well-chronicled in the financial reviews.' She kept her eyes steady, and she even managed a faint smile. 'Likewise, your social activities are reported in the tabloid Press.' She paused, then allowed her gaze to rove carefully over his superb frame. 'You're obviously in good health . . .' She trailed off, and effected a slight shrug. 'I'm sure we can spare each other a rundown of our respective love lives.'

For a brief milli-second his eyes resembled dark ice, then soft, husky laughter emerged from his throat, and unless she was mistaken there was a degree of brooding respect evident in the glance he spared her.

'You've grown up,' he drawled lazily, and pain momentarily clouded her eyes.

'At twenty-five, one would hope so,' she responded sweetly.

'I promised Paige I'd take you straight to the hospital,' Dimitri said minutes later as he eased the car off the freeway.

A chill fear clutched her heart, and she searched his chiselled features for a hint of reassurance, and found none. It was two months since she'd seen her mother, and she agonised that she hadn't detected even a glimmer of concern in Paige's voice, a slight hesitancy—anything that might have betrayed a glimpse of anxiety relevant to a worrying health problem.

How could such a thing happen? she raged silently. Paige ate all the right foods, exercised and played tennis, never smoked, and drank minimally. *Why*?

Ten minutes later the Jaguar swung through open wrought-iron gates and traversed a wide, pebbled driveway to park at the rear of one of Melbourne's most exclusive private hospitals.

As they passed through Reception the nurse spared Dimitri a smile tinged with a degree of wistful envy, whereas the sister in charge had no such qualms.

'Mrs Kostakidas is resting quite comfortably.' Her eyes held liquid warmth and a silent invitation, should the man at Leanne's side choose to give the merest indication of interest.

Leanne watched with detached resignation, and wondered whether her exalted stepbrother would choose to make another conquest. In his late thirties, he was an intensely sensual man whose power, wealth and sheer physicality drew women like bees to a honeypot. Yet he had a select coterie of women friends with whom he chose to dine and indulge in social proclivities. Inevitably, there were some he surely bedded, but not, she suspected, indiscriminately. A newsprint photo taken at a recent glitzy function came vividly to mind; it had named his female companion as Shanna Delahunty, only daughter of Reginald Delahunty, the insurance magnate.

'Paige's suite is to the right.'

The quietly spoken words served as a timely warning, for they gave Leanne the few essential seconds necessary to seek control before she walked into the luxurious suite.

Despite having been given the grim medical facts, Leanne found it impossible to relate the gaunt, pale-featured woman lying propped against a nest of pillows with her mother.

It wasn't easy to smile, and it took a tremendous strength of will to keep the tears at bay as she crossed to the bed and carefully embraced the slight figure. Paige's bones appeared fragile, and her skin felt like fine tissue paper. It was if the essence of her mother had gone, and Leanne wanted to scream out against the unkind hand of fate.

'Hello, darling.' The words were softly spoken, the smile truly beautiful, as if the flickering flame deep within had gained a small measure of renewed life. A hand lifted, and faintly trembling fingers brushed the length of Leanne's cheek. 'I'm so glad you're here.'

The desire to weep was almost irrepressible, and Leanne gave a slight start as Dimitri curved an arm round her shoulders. His silent strength acted as a protective cloak, and she stood perfectly still, her features carefully schooled as Paige feasted her eyes lovingly on her daughter's diminutive frame before shifting to the man at her side.

'Thank you.' The words were a soft whisper, and Dimitri's eyes were dark, liquid with affection, yet when they slid towards Leanne they became vaguely smoky in silent warning, and she stiffened fractionally as his fingers shifted and began a subtle massage of the fine bones at the edge of her shoulder.

'We'll leave you to rest,' he said as he leant forward to brush Paige's cheek with his lips. 'Leanne will call in after lunch, and we'll both visit this evening.'

'Yes.'

Paige's voice was barely audible, and Leanne managed to contain her tears until they were in the corridor, then they spilled over and began trickling in twin rivulets down each cheek.

The corridor seemed longer than she remembered, and by the time she slid into the passenger seat she was an emotional wreck.

'Why didn't I know she was ill?' Leanne demanded with a mixture of impotent rage and deep anguish, then, as a thought occurred to her, she turned towards the man who had just slid in behind the wheel. 'Why didn't *you* tell me?'

'Simply because I didn't know,' Dimitri assured her hardly. 'Paige and I maintain weekly telephone contact, and I dine at the house every few weeks.'

In between business trips that took him from one Australian state capital to another, and numerous countries around the world, his base was a spacious penthouse suite atop a stylish apartment block barely two kilometres distant from his late father's Toorak mansion.

'Paige showed no signs of illness? Nothing?' Leanne queried with disbelief.

'I last saw her five weeks ago, and, although pale, she assured me she was recuperating well from a virulent flu virus.' His eyes were dark, his expression reflective. 'I left the next day for a series of meetings in the States, then Paris, Rome, followed by a stop-over in Perth. A fax from Paige's medical adviser was waiting for me at the hotel,' he relayed bleakly. 'I rang you as soon as I had all the facts.'

'She must have suspected something, surely?' Leanne agonised huskily.

'The medical professionals informed me she's been aware of the severity of her condition for several months. It was her express wish to keep it private until such time as she required hospitalisation.'

Her throat felt painfully constricted, and she was barely managing to keep the tears at bay. Dammit, where was the slim pack of tissues she always carried? Moisture spilled over and ran down her cheeks, and her fingers shook as she brushed the tears away.

She heard his unintelligible oath, then a soft white square was pushed into her hand and he pulled her into the protective curve of his shoulder.

Her initial instinct was to move away, but she lacked sufficient strength to break free. Tears streamed silently down her cheeks and dampened his shirt, and she was vaguely aware of his fingers slipping beneath the weight of her hair to trace a soothing pattern across a collection of fragile bones.

She had no idea how long she remained there before she regained a measure of control. Only minutes, surely, she agonised despairingly

'I'm sorry,' she profferred in a slightly muffled voice as she attempted to pull free.

'For what, Leanne?' he drawled in cynical query. 'Dropping your guard long enough to accept my compassion?'

'I didn't——'

'Want to display any emotion in my presence?'

'No,' she retaliated bleakly, unwilling to show so much as a chink in her armour. She sat still and stared sightlessly out of the window, remembering all too vividly the numerous occasions when she'd deliberately sought his attention. Attention he'd affectionately fielded without hurting her vulnerable feelings, until the fateful night of her twenty-first birthday.

Leanne closed her eyes in an attempt to shut out a memory that was hauntingly clear in every detail.

Paige had provided a wonderful party with many invited friends, and Leanne had been so happy. No guest had been more important to her than Dimitri, and the secret wish she'd nursed that at last he would recognise her as a woman. Flushed with a dangerous sense of exhilaration, she'd flirted a little with every male friend, and enjoyed one glass too many of vintage champagne. At the end of the evening, when everyone had left and Paige had retired upstairs to bed, she'd reactivated the stereo system, selected a tape and teasingly begged Dimitri to share a dance.

Emboldened, she'd pressed her body a little too close to his and lifted her arms to clasp them around his nape. The top of her head had barely reached his chin, and she'd arched her neck, offered him a bewitching smile and teased that he had yet to bestow a birthday kiss.

It had begun as a teasing salutation, and had rapidly transgressed to something so infinitely sensual that she had simply discarded any inhibitions and given herself up to an exotic alchemy without any clear thought as to where it might lead.

She'd had no idea of the passage of time until she had been forcibly put at arm's length, and his harsh words had sent her running upstairs to her bedroom to weep until almost dawn.

The next day he'd flown to Sydney, and during the ensuing weeks she had convinced Paige of the necessity to exert a new-found independence away from home, electing, despite Paige's protests, to choose Queensland's Gold Coast as her base.

Paige had become a frequent visitor, and Leanne had carefully arranged her weekends and holidays in Melbourne to coincide with Dimitri's absence, although it had been impossible to avoid him completely. If he was on the Coast, he made a point of phoning and insisting on taking her out to dinner, or to a show, or both... in the guise of dutiful, stepbrotherly affection. His invitations had become a challenge she coolly accepted, for she refused to give him the satisfaction of knowing he still possessed the ability to ruffle her composure.

'Paige is a rare jewel who succeeded in capturing my father's heart, affording me unconditional affection without attempting to usurp Yanis's loyalty to his son.' Dimitri's voice intruded, and she turned her head to look at him. '*You*,' he added with quiet emphasis, 'were an added bonus.'

Latent anger rose to the surface and threatened to erupt in speech. 'You . . .' Words momentarily failed her. 'Bastard,' she finally flung in whispered anguish. It was the wrong appellation, and, worse, an unforgivable insult. But at that precise moment she didn't care.

The silence in the car was deafening, and she could sense his palpable anger. For a second she closed her eyes against the harshness of his features, then slowly opened them again.

Dimitri activated the ignition, then reversed out of the parking bay, and the crunch of tyres sounded abnormally loud as he eased the car towards the designated exit.

The exclusive suburb of Toorak hosted numerous homes belonging to the rich and famous, and the elegant residence that Yanis had built was no exception, she decided as Dimitri brought the Jaguar to a halt before a set of impressive wrought-iron gates, then activated the remote-control modem to open them.

The car swept down a wide, palm-lined driveway and drew to a halt beneath the *porte cochère* of a magnificent Mediterranean-style mansion whose white-rendered exterior and terracotta-tiled roof conjured up images of the hillside vineyard estates of the Côte d'Azur.

A grandly proportioned home, it contained over a hundred square feet of luxury living on two levels, with five bedrooms and six bathrooms in the main house, a guest cabana which included a lounge and bar, a free-form swimming-pool and a full-size tennis court.

Scrupulously maintained, its gracious formal rooms had been used to entertain Yanis's business associates, and family friends. A generous man, he'd lent his name to a few worthy charities, and a small fortune in much needed funds had been raised through a variety of functions held here over the years.

Leanne slid from the car, then followed Dimitri through double leadlight doors to the formal entrance hall—a stately marble-tiled room with a crystal chandelier and sweeping mahogany staircase.

Although it had been her home for the past ten years, Leanne never failed to experience a feeling of awe at the sheer magnificence of displayed wealth.

Cream marble-tiled floors graced the ground floor, and there was an abundance of expensive Chinese silk rugs woven in designs employing mushroom, pink, pale blue and green against a cream background. Expensive tapestries graced the pale cream silk-covered walls, and vied for supremacy with original works of art. Yanis had indulged Paige her love of Louis XVI furnishings, and much of the furniture had been imported from France and Italy.

Now a chill slowly traversed the length of Leanne's spine, and she had consciously to still the sudden shiver that threatened to shake her slender frame with the knowledge that, although Yanis had bequeathed this beautiful mansion to Paige for her exclusive use during her lifetime, upon her death it would inevitably revert to his son.

Which meant that within weeks Leanne would no longer be able to regard it as her home, for afterwards she knew she wouldn't be able to bear seeing Dimitri here with the woman he would inevitably choose to take as his wife.

It shouldn't be too difficult to reduce contact gradually to an occasional telephone call, a few brief, friendly written missives, followed by a card at Christmas.

'Leanne, it is so good to see you.'

A heavily accented voice broke into her reverie, and she turned at once to exchange a warm greeting with Eleni Takis—cook and housekeeper who, together with her husband George, took care of the house and grounds.

'Eleni.' There was evidence of barely contained tears, and a wealth of genuine affection.

'George will take up your luggage,' Eleni declared as she stood back. 'And lunch will be ready in thirty minutes.'

'You shouldn't have gone to any trouble,' Leanne protested, knowing she'd have difficulty in consuming more than a few mouthfuls of anything.

'Nonsense,' Eleni admonished, and her appraisal of Leanne's slender frame became faintly critical. 'You have lost weight. In one so small, that is not good.'

'If I ate even a half of what you served me, I'd go back to the Coast half a stone heavier and one dress size larger.'

Eleni looked slightly perplexed. 'But this time you stay. Yes?'

'Any messages, Eleni?' Dimitri drawled, and Leanne intercepted an unspoken warning in his tone.

'Your secretary rang. She is sending you faxes.'

Leanne shot him a quick, enquiring glance as Eleni departed, and met his dark, discerning gaze.

'Paige requested I take up temporary residence, as she didn't want you to be in the house on your own.'

Her stomach churned at the thought of having to live, even for a short time, in such close proximity to a man with whom she felt the antithesis of comfortable.

She drew a deep breath, then exhaled it slowly as she sought to keep her voice light. 'I fail to see why, when I've lived alone for the past five years. Besides, Eleni and George live above the garages.'

His eyes narrowed fractionally. 'Go upstairs and unpack. We'll talk over lunch.'

About *what*, for heaven's sake?

Her bedroom was spacious, airy, and had a splendid view of the pool and gardens. The muted colour scheme was restful, the furniture the epitome of elegance with its imported silk upholstery, and the adjoining *en-suite* bathroom was a feminine delight in the palest pink travertine marble with crystal and gold fittings.

Without further thought, she discarded her clothes and stepped into the shower cubicle, emerging minutes later to select elegant trousers and a top in pale sage-green cotton, then, dressed, she tended to her hair and make-up.

It was almost one when she entered the kitchen, and Eleni cast her a warm smile.

'You are just in time. Everything is ready, except for the bread.'

'I'll take it through,' Leanne offered promptly as she crossed to the oven. 'Anything else?'

'Just the lamb. The salads are on the table.'

It looked like a feast fit for a king, and far more than two people could possibly eat. There was chilled wine resting in a silver bucket, two exquisite crystal flutes, silver cutlery and the finest bone china.

Eleni took extreme pride in the house, preparing food and presenting a fine table. Paige was a gracious employer who attested that material possessions were useless if they reposed in cupboards and cabinets merely for visual display.

Dimitri entered the room within minutes, smiled indulgently at Eleni's fussing, then took a seat opposite Leanne as the older woman retreated to the kitchen.

'Wine?'

'No—thank you,' Leanne refused with the utmost politeness.

'The keys to Paige's Mercedes are in the top drawer of the cabinet in the foyer,' he informed her as he filled his glass.

'Thank you.'

His eyes narrowed slightly. 'You're hardly a guest, Leanne. The car, or anything else you need, is at your disposal.'

She was about to utter thanks for the third time, then opted against it, choosing instead to attempt to do justice to the excellent Greek salad Eleni had prepared.

Perhaps if she concentrated on food, this crazy ambivalence would disappear. It was quite mad, but she felt as if she was teetering on the edge of a precipice, and nothing could shake her acute feeling of apprehension.

Overwrought, overtired and consumed with anxiety—all of which was quite logical in light of her mother's state of health, she qualified as she speared a segment of feta cheese and attacked an olive.

The delicately roasted lamb fared little better, and she forked a few mouthfuls then pushed the remaining meat and accompanying vegetables round her plate before discarding it completely.

'Not hungry?'

'Eleni will disapprove,' she offered ruefully.

Dimitri pushed his napkin on to the table and leaned back in his chair. 'Relax, Leanne.' His eyes were dark, enigmatic, yet there was a tinge of mockery evident.

'What topic would you suggest we politely pursue? The state of the nation, the weather? Your latest property acquisition?'

'Paige,' he insisted quietly. 'Her wishes, and what we intend to do about them.'

Dear lord, he didn't pull any punches—just aimed straight for the jugular. 'There isn't a thing I wouldn't do to please her,' she assured him without hesitation.

'Without exception?'

She didn't need to think. 'Of course.'

Dimitri regarded her in silence for several long seconds, his gaze infinitely speculative beneath faintly hooded lids. 'Even assuming the pretence of a romantic alliance with me?'

CHAPTER TWO

FOR an instant Leanne was robbed of the power of speech, then the colour drained from her face, leaving it pale.

'I don't find that suggestion very amusing,' she said at last.

Dimitri's eyes never left hers, their dark depths faintly brooding, and she had the instinctive feeling that he had already weighed all the angles and was intent on playing a manipulative game.

'I'm perfectly serious.'

The breath seemed suddenly locked in her throat, and she swallowed compulsively in the need to regain her voice. '*Why?*'

'Paige is concerned for your future,' he offered, noting the faint wariness which was apparent.

Logic vied with rationale, then mingled with a degree of angry resentment. 'I've lived an independent life for more than four years. My future is secure, and afterwards...' She trailed to a halt, then forced herself to continue. 'I'll simply return to the Coast.'

'Where you'll become an easy prey for fortune hunters,' Dimitri accorded indolently.

'Don't be ridiculous,' she denied at once. 'This house, everything, will revert to you.'

'The house, yes. However, there are annuities you will inherit from a number of Kostakidas-affiliated corporations. There's also an apartment in Athens, a home in Switzerland, and a villa in France. Jewellery, stocks, shares. Gifts Yanis bestowed on Paige during his lifetime. All of which will become yours.' He paused slightly, watching her expressive features carefully as the effect of his words sank in. 'Added together, their worth totals several million.'

It was almost impossible to comprehend, for, although she'd known her late stepfather's personal wealth had been measured in millions, she'd had no idea of its extent. It wasn't something she or Paige had ever discussed.

'Yanis gifted me the Gold Coast apartment, and the beauty clinic,' she said at once, perturbed beyond rational thought. 'I don't want or need anything else.'

'Those weren't my father's wishes. Nor,' he added quietly, 'are they mine.'

'I'll contest Paige's will in your favour,' she declared vehemently.

'Impossible. That eventuality has already been foreseen and legally negated.'

'It can all accumulate and be held in trust.'

His smile held a tinge of cynicism. 'Idealistic, Leanne, but scarcely practical.' He regarded her carefully. 'Paige and Yanis nurtured the hope that we might eventually become romantically attached, and it would give Paige peace of mind to believe that their fondest wish has eventuated. As it is, she's consumed with anxiety over the men who will beat a path to your door, professing undying love in order to enjoy a free meal-ticket for life.'

Her eyes widened, their blue depths darkening measurably as she wrestled with a desire to please her mother and the fear that she'd never emerge from such subterfuge unscathed.

'I'm no longer fifteen, and I do possess a degree of common sense. I don't think I need a protector.' Not you, she added silently. Dear lord, never you.

'We're discussing Paige,' he reminded her, with velvet softness.

'I don't want to deceive her,' she offered slowly.

'Yet you love her very much,' he pursued, and she shivered inwardly. 'Enough to enter into a pretence that will make her happy, and ensure her peace of mind?'

'What do you want, Dimitri? My unequivocal agreement to enact a lie?'

His eyes hardened fractionally, and his mouth curved to form a wry smile. 'Will it prove so difficult given the limited time-span?'

She closed her eyes, then slowly opened them. 'You know how to twist the knife, don't you?' she countered with a trace of bitterness.

His gaze didn't falter as he reached for his glass. 'Will you have some fruit, or would you prefer coffee?'

How could he sit there and switch so calmly from something of such personal magnitude to a mundane selection over lunch? Even as she contemplated the silent query, the answer followed. Dimitri was an astute businessman, well-versed in the cut and thrust utilised by power-brokers all over the world. He clinched deals worth millions, dealt with hardliners in the financial arena, and undoubtedly annihilated lesser minions on a day-to-day basis. Against such a formidable force, what chance did she have?

'Chilled water,' Leanne indicated, viewing him with circumspection as he took the carafe and re-filled her glass.

'Tell me about the beauty clinic,' he encouraged with apparent interest, and she suffered his appraisal with unblinking solemnity, all too aware of what he saw, for it was an image she knew in detail.

Pale, fine-textured skin, a delicate bone-structure, a wide, generous mouth framing even white teeth, a nondescript nose, wide-spaced deep blue eyes, and shoulder-length natural ash-blonde hair.

'It's successful,' she dismissed with a negligible shrug. 'Women like to look good, and most are prepared to spend money in the name of beauty.'

'Merely for self-gratification?'

'Of course. And pleasing a man.' She could recall instantly the features of several socialites who devoted much of their morning hours on a regular basis to one beauty treatment or another. Aromatherapy, a facial, brow- and lash-tinting, massage, waxing, manicure and pedicure, to mention a few. When that failed to revive the passage of nature satisfactorily, they resorted to the skill of cosmetic surgery. Chasing elusive beauty and maintaining it was an expensive pastime, and Leanne was a skilled beautician, dedicated to her craft.

Dimitri reached forward and extracted a peach from the fruit bowl which he proceeded to peel and stone before offering her a segment. 'No?'

The need to be free of his disturbing presence was overwhelming, and she excused herself from the table.

'I'll be caught up in the city for most of the afternoon,' he revealed as she got to her feet. 'Be ready at six. We'll visit Paige, then go on somewhere for dinner.'

Leanne was unable to resist the query. 'Won't Shanna object?'

His gaze was remarkably level. 'Shanna has nothing to do with my taking you to dinner.'

'You could always drop me home, then meet her later.'

'This conversation is going nowhere, Leanne,' Dimitri drawled hatefully.

'In that case, I'll give Eleni a hand clearing the table, unpack, then visit Paige,' she returned with the utmost politeness, and his husky laughter made her want to lash out in anger. Except that such an action would invoke his temper, and she'd already insulted him. To do so again on the same day would be the height of folly.

It was almost two-thirty when Leanne entered her mother's suite and her heart contracted as Paige complimented gently, 'Darling, you look so well.'

What could she say in return? It was difficult, much more difficult than she'd envisaged, and she simply pulled a chair close to the bed and sat holding Paige's hand.

'Dimitri is very fond of you,' Paige offered huskily. Perhaps medication had eased her pain, for she didn't seem to be under quite so much strain. 'Anything you need, he'll advise and guide you. He's given me his word.'

Leanne wanted to cry, and her vision began to shimmer with the onset of tears. Oh, dear God, she agonised, *help* me.

'Yanis loved you so much, almost as much as I do. He adored having you as his daughter.'

'He was a wonderful man.'

'Yes,' Paige agreed simply. 'As is his son.'

No. The single negation was a silent scream which seemed to reverberate inside her brain. Don't do this to me. She longed to say that Dimitri had been the embodiment of her fantasy hero, as seen through the eyes of a teenage child. Her problem was in discovering he had feet of clay.

'Everything I have will be yours. Property, jewellery,' Paige continued after a long pause. 'It amounts to a very sizeable inheritance, darling.'

Leanne felt her chest tighten with emotional pain, and her throat began to constrict as she attempted to gain some control over her turbulent emotions. 'I don't think I want to talk about it. It hurts too much,' she whispered.

'But I'm not afraid. Really,' Paige assured her gently, her eyes a soft blue without any hint of fear. 'My beloved Yanis will be there. And I don't want you to be sad.' Her eyes misted, and her lips curved into a soft, tremulous smile. 'If I could have one wish, it would be to see you happily settled with a man who will love and care for you. Marriage,' she continued quietly, and her fingers stroked Leanne's hand with an absent, abstracted movement. 'And children.'

Grandchildren you'll never have the pleasure of seeing, Leanne said silently. It wasn't fair. Paige would have made a wonderful grandmother.

Leanne was aware that any moment now she'd burst into tears. 'I am happy,' she said quickly. Too quickly. Paige's illness and level of medication hadn't diminished her perceptiveness in any way.

'Are you, darling?'

Unable to find any adequate words that wouldn't sound defensive, Leanne offered a shaky smile and launched into an amusing anecdote about something that had happened at the clinic. Then she left Paige to rest for an hour, and returned briefly with some of her mother's favourite roses as well as some fresh fruit in the hope of tempting her appetite.

It was almost five when she arrived home, and after alerting Eleni that she was back she moved swiftly upstairs, shed her clothes, donned a swimsuit and then made her way down to the pool.

Perhaps if she set herself a rigorous number of lengths she would be able to dispel the haunting image of her mother's pale features and the infinite sadness beneath her gentle smile.

It didn't work; nor did attempting to focus her thoughts elsewhere. Consequently she was feeling infinitely fragile when she descended the stairs a few minutes before six.

Dimitri was in the lounge, a tall glass of chilled water in one hand, and his dark eyes speared hers as she entered the room.

'A cool drink?' He indicated a crystal water-pitcher liberally filled with ice-cubes and decorated with sliced lemon and sprigs of mint.

'Please.'

He took a glass and filled it, then handed it to her, his expression musingly speculative as she carefully avoided touching his fingers.

He looked what he was: a well-educated man, well-versed in the analysis of humankind and aware of the limits of his control. It was a mantle he wore with uncontrived ease, and she felt a thousand light-years removed from his particular brand of sophistication. Which was crazy, especially as she'd been privy to an elevated lifestyle during the past ten years, and could converse knowledgeably on a variety of subjects.

It was Dimitri himself who unsettled her, for his degree of sensuality was a heady, potent entity she constantly fought against, aware that if she were ever to lose her inner battle the results would be totally cataclysmic.

He subjected her to an thorough appraisal, then let his gaze rest thoughtfully on the contoured pink fullness of her mouth.

'When you've finished, we'll leave.'

In the car he slotted a cassette into the stereo system and concentrated on negotiating the early evening traffic. Leanne conjured up a number of conversational subjects to pursue, only to discard each one, and she sat quietly as the sleek, powerful vehicle ate up the distance.

Paige had already eaten, and she brightened as Leanne preceded Dimitri into the room.

'You look lovely, darling,' Paige complimented her gently. 'That shade of blue does wonderful things for your eyes.' Her gaze shifted to the man at her daughter's side. 'Don't you think so?'

'Stunning,' Dimnitri agreed as he crossed to the bed and brushed his lips against Paige's temple. 'How are you feeling?'

There was such a depth of affectionate concern in his voice that Leanne's body quivered slightly, and she was conscious that her voice sounded a little too bright as she greeted her mother, then sank into a chair which Dimitri had pulled close to the bed.

He merely stood close behind her. Much too close. She was conscious of him with every muscle in her body, every nerve-end, and it was all she could do not to visibly jump when his hand came to rest on her shoulder.

Paige noticed the implied intimacy, and smiled. 'Where are you going for dinner?'

He named a restaurant that was not only ruinously expensive, but well-known for its fine cuisine.

Paige's eyes took on a luminous sheen. 'Is it a celebration of some kind?'

'Not quite,' Dimitri drawled, and Leanne felt his fingers tighten slightly over the fine bones at the edge of her collarbone. 'I'm hopeful that the combination of an excellent vintage wine and superb food will persuade Leanne to accept my proposal.'

The air became trapped in her lungs, impeding her breathing, and she could have sworn that the beat of her heart stopped before it went racing into overdrive. Words froze in her throat as he curved his free hand round the sensitive arch of her nape.

You bastard, she longed to cry out at him. An angry denial rushed to her lips, then died as she caught sight of her mother's expression.

Joy, pure joyous relief intermingled with a happiness so vivid it lit her features and turned them into something so incredibly beautiful that it brought any verbal negation that Leanne might have uttered to a halt.

As Dimitri had known it would. Just as he knew she wouldn't have the heart to do anything other than go to her mother's outstretched arms and accept the loving embrace, share her tears, then watch with a sense of stunned disbelief as Dimitri extracted a slim pouch and slid a large, pear-shaped diamond on to the appropriate finger of her left hand.

'You didn't breathe a word this afternoon,' Paige said huskily.

'Quite simply because I had no idea of Dimitri's intention,' Leanne responded with a calm she was far from feeling. The ring felt heavy, and she barely resisted the temptation to tear it from her finger.

'Yanis would have been so happy. As I am.' Her mother's words were faintly breathy, emotion-filled, and somehow Leanne managed a suitable response.

Presenting the façade of a newly engaged fiancée took all her acting ability, and it was a minor miracle that she managed to emerge almost forty minutes later from Paige's suite without having resorted to histrionics.

Leanne was silent all the way to the car, and she didn't utter a word as he reversed out of the car park and eased the vehicle on to the main thoroughfare, then her tightly controlled anger erupted in a heated flow of words designed to blister his hateful hide.

'How *dare* you?'

'Pre-empt your decision? It was a foregone conclusion, knowing the depth of your love for Paige.'

'That doesn't give you the right——'

'I care for Paige very much. Enough to give her pleasure for what limited time she has left. Surely we can put aside our own differences long enough to perpetuate an illusion?'

'That isn't the point!'

'What is the point, Leanne? Your resentment, your anger? Surely the focus should be Paige herself?'

She was too incensed to accede to his dictum, and she flung furiously, 'I don't want to have dinner with you.'

'I've made a reservation, and we both need to eat. Why not share a meal together?'

'Because I'm so mad, I'll probably pick up the soup plate and tip the contents over your head!'

'I shall consider myself forewarned.'

'Or the salad,' she muttered direly as he pulled into a car park adjacent to one of Toorak's well-known restaurants.

The ring was an alien manacle, and she slid it off, ready to hand it to him the instant he cut the ignition.

'Leave it on,' Dimitri ordered as she thrust it at him.

'*Why?*'

'It stays on, Leanne.'

'Don't be ridiculous. It's far too valuable, and too——' She had been going to say beautiful, because the stone in its setting was exquisite. 'Everyone will notice.'

'Precisely,' he conceded with dry cynicism, and her eyes widened in shocked disbelief.

'You mean to go public with this?'

'Paige has a phone beside her bed,' he enlightened her. 'Her weakened state doesn't prevent her from making calls.' He viewed Leanne's dawning horror with musing cynicism. 'It will take only one friend to spread the news and within a matter of days it will have circulated among the social set.'

'You really mean to go through with this pretence *openly*?'

'Of course. It has to be seen to succeed.'

'Define *succeed*, Dimitri,' she insisted, aware that the whole thing was rapidly getting out of hand. Like a snowball accumulating in size as it gained momentum and assumed the very real threat of becoming an avalanche.

'A formal announcement in the Press tomorrow.'

'You mean you've actually gone that far?' Her voice rose. 'You damned egotistical, proprietorial *bastard*!'

'Watch your unwary tongue,' he warned silkily.

'Forgive me,' Leanne flung with unaccustomed sarcasm. 'I wasn't aware I shouldn't put up any resistance to a scheme I'm not happy with—*or*,' she added vengefully, 'dare to upbraid you for taking charge without my sanction.'

'Come and eat.'

'I don't want to eat, and I especially don't want to eat with you.'

'Nevertheless, you will.'

'I refuse to sit at the same table and *pretend*. The food would choke me.'

'Aren't you being overly dramatic?'

'Don't patronise me, Dimitri,' she said darkly.

'You used to be such an obedient child,' he relayed musingly.

'What would you know?' she flung. 'You were rarely there.'

'Did you want me to be?'

That was too close to the bone for comfort, and her eyes were startlingly clear in the subdued overhead lighting. 'You were thirteen years my senior, more sophisticated, and a thousand light-years ahead of me. Besides, a teenage stepsister would have cramped your style.'

'Yet there were occasions when I partnered you to several functions Paige and Yanis chose to attend,' he alluded with deceptive mildness.

She remembered them well, each one etched permanently in her brain. Now she felt resentful that he'd adroitly defused the immediate situation by orchestrating a subtle shift from her heated anger.

'This restaurant is one of your favourite haunts,' she reminded him stoically, then added the rider, 'What if Shanna is there?'

'We're all civilised adults,' Dimitri returned smoothly.

'This—this *farce*,' she said in a tight voice, 'is solely for Paige's benefit. If you dare to act out the part of adoring fiancé anywhere else but at the hospital——'

'Difficult to confine our actions, when it will be news in a variety of papers tomorrow,' he drawled.

'I'll never forgive you,' she vowed with renewed vehemence.

'Our first public appearance *à deux* is inevitable,' he told her drily. 'Besides, what excuse will you give Paige for a change in plan? That we couldn't wait to be alone together?'

She barely restrained herself from hitting out at him, and angry resolve prompted her to reach for the door-catch. 'Do you always use such devious tactics in a bid to achieve your objective?'

She didn't wait to hear his answer, and slid out from the passenger seat, choosing to walk on ahead of him. A fruitless exercise, for she'd scarcely taken half a dozen steps before he reached her side.

The restaurant was one she'd frequented occasionally with Paige, and its elegant décor projected an ambience that was frequently sought by the city's upper social echelons. Which was probably why Dimitri had selected it, she decided darkly as the *maître d'* proffered an effusive greeting before leading them to a prominent table reserved, Leanne instantly surmised, for the chosen, favoured few.

Dimitri ordered champagne, Dom Pérignon, and at Leanne's faintly raised eyebrow he merely smiled and asked the wine steward to fill her glass.

The lighting was subdued and attuned to intimate dining, but she felt as if she and Dimitri were the room's central focus. The diamond on her finger flashed with a fiery brilliance from myriad facets, and she pushed her hand out of sight on her lap, supremely conscious of its significance.

The restaurant catered for leisurely dining, and she selected the soup *de jour*, followed it with a prawn starter, refused a main course, passed on dessert and opted against the cheeseboard. The serving of each course seemed to take an age, and by the time coffee was brought to the table she was seething with impatience to leave.

To attempt to maintain a polite façade almost killed her, yet inherent good manners wouldn't permit a public display of anger.

And he knew, damn him, for he kept up a *divertissement* that was masterly, with an ease she could only admire but inwardly seethe at as he tempted her to try a morsel from his fork and refilled her flute with champagne.

The coffee was strong and aromatic, and she sipped it abstractedly, wishing only for the evening to conclude. She was tired, emotionally exhausted, and suffering the onset of a headache.

A predominate waft—*wave*, Leanne corrected wryly—of exotic perfume assailed her nostrils, and was immediately followed by the tinkling sound of a feminine voice.

'Dimitri, what *are* you doing here? I understood you weren't due back from Perth until next week.'

'Shanna.' Dimitri's greeting was warm, but not effusive.

Courtesy ensured an acknowledgement of his companion. 'Leanne.' The brunette proffered a brilliant smile. 'How are you? Are you down on holiday from the Coast?'

'Not exactly,' Leanne managed in polite response.

'Is this a family tête-à-tête? Or may I join you?'

'Leanne and I were just about to leave,' Dimitri imparted smoothly.

'Surely you could stay,' Shanna suggested persuasively. 'There's a group of us, just friends—we'd love you to join us.'

'Thank you—but not tonight.'

The *maître d'* hovered discreetly as Dimitri signed the credit slip, then moved unobtrusively out of sight.

Shanna's eyes moved to the empty champagne bottle. 'Celebrating a recent success, darling?'

'You could say that,' he responded, shooting Leanne a musing smile. 'Personal, not business.'

'You've aroused my curiosity. Is it confidential?'

'I've persuaded Leanne to marry me.'

Shanna's smile slipped for the space of a second, and Leanne could only commend her superb control, for, although the brunette's features portrayed surprised pleasure, her eyes held a darkness that contained bitter disappointment.

'You must tell me how you managed to convince Dimitri to make a commitment,' she said to Leanne.

A degree of humour was the only way, and Leanne tempered her reply with a musing smile. 'He simply slid a ring on my finger.'

Dimitri stood and held out his hand to Leanne. 'You'll excuse us, Shanna?'

Leanne had no recourse but to follow his lead, and she felt a certain sympathy for the attractive model. Rejection hurt like hell. Hadn't she suffered at Dimitri's hands more than four years ago? As she would again, a tiny voice taunted. How long after Paige's passing would he retract the engagement—a few days, a week?

'You've burned your bridges,' Leanne said as the Jaguar picked up a cruising speed, and she incurred Dimitri's dark glance.

'There were no bridges to burn,' he replied with deliberate mockery.

'She was your——' She couldn't say it.

'Lover?' he prompted.

'Yes!'

'We visited the opera on a few occasions, took in the theatre, and attended several parties and functions.'

'I don't care what you did together.'

'No?'

'You could have bedded a hundred women, for all I care.'

'I'm very particular as to who shares my bed.'

She was unable to resist the taunt, 'I'm not the one you should be attempting to reassure.'

He didn't answer, and there was something heady about having the last word. It lifted her spirits, and prompted an appraisal of her surroundings.

A dark indigo sky with a sprinkling of stars was at variance with the light summer shower that was as sudden as it was fleeting, necessitating only a few swishing turns of the wiper blades. Bright neon street-lights provided intermittent illumination, and cast long, deepening shadows from numerous trees standing guard on both sides of the suburban road.

There was the slight but distinctive sound of tyre-treads traversing wet bitumen, then the car slowed and paused as Dimitri activated the remote-control module that electronically opened the gates.

Within minutes another button released the garage doors, and the Jaguar slid to a halt between Paige's Mercedes and a luxurious four-wheel drive.

Once inside, Leanne made her way towards the stairs.

'Will you join me in a nightcap?'

'No,' she declared evenly. 'I'm going to bed. I'm tired and I have a headache.'

'I'm disappointed,' he said with studied indolence. 'I imagined the instant we reached the house you'd fly at me in a rage.'

'I want to,' Leanne assured him tightly. 'Badly. Unfortunately I don't possess the energy to launch an attack.'

A slight smile curved his mouth, and there was a gleam apparent in his dark gaze. 'In that case, I'll see you at breakfast.'

The words she wanted to hurl at him remained unsaid, and she ascended the stairs to her room where she undressed and removed her make-up before slipping between the cool, freshly laundered sheets.

She should have fallen asleep the instant her head touched the pillow. Instead, her mind was filled with a host of images, not the least being Paige herself, and the inimicable man who had temporarily taken charge of her life.

She had little comprehension of how long she lay staring at the darkened ceiling as the painful throbbing in her head deepened until she began to feel physically ill. Her body broke out in a sweat, then began to cool, and she knew any attempt at sleep without some form of medication would be useless.

Slipping out of bed, she crossed to the *en-suite* bathroom and rummaged through the bathroom cabinet for some pain-killers, only to curse softly on discovering that there were none.

She lifted a hand and pressed it wearily against her temple. Maybe there was something in the cabinet in Paige's suite. If not, she'd have to venture downstairs.

It took only a few minutes to discover that there was nothing stronger available than paracetamol, and she closed her eyes momentarily, then opened them again in restrained exasperation. Maybe if she took two now it would take the edge off the pain sufficiently so that she could sleep.

There was a tumbler on the marble-topped vanity unit, and she half filled it with water only to have it slip through her fingers and crash down into the marbled basin.

'Dear God,' she whispered shakily at the explosive sound of shattering glass. It was enough to wake the dead. The last thing she needed was to have to face Dimitri at this hour of the night.

Yet he appeared in the doorway within seconds, his features dark and forbidding.

She could visualise the scene through his eyes. A slight figure attired in a long cotton nightshirt, dishevelled hair, and pale features overshadowed by large eyes darkened with pain.

'I'm sorry the noise woke you.' Her eyes felt heavy and impossibly bruised. She lifted a hand, then let it fall helplessly down to her side. 'I'll pick up the glass.'

'Leave it,' Dimitri instructed brusquely. 'Eleni can attend to it in the morning.' His eyes swept to the foil strip of tablets, then to her pale features. 'Headache worse?'

'Yes.' She winced painfully, closing her eyes against his forceful image and the degree of sexual magnetism he exuded. The white towelling robe he'd hastily donned merely enhanced his height and breadth, and she was in no fit state to arm a mental defence against him. 'I'll just take these, then go back to bed.'

Without a word he leaned forward, extracted another tumbler, half filled it with water, then placed it in her hand.

When she'd swallowed the tablets, she replaced the tumbler, then made to move past him only to give a gasp of surprise as he leaned forward and lifted her into his arms.

'Put me down.' The protest was adamant, for the shift in gravity had caused her nightshirt to ride dangerously up her thighs, and she was acutely conscious of a loss of modesty.

His strength was palpable, and this close she could smell the faint muskiness of his skin mingling with a trace of aftershave. She had only to turn her head fractionally for her lips to come in contact with the edge of his neck.

'I can walk. There's nothing wrong with my legs.' Even a severe headache couldn't diminish the heightened degree of sensual awareness she felt at being held so close against him. 'Put me down!'

'Why so nervous?' Dimitri queried lazily as he gained the hallway and headed towards her suite.

'You're enjoying this, aren't you?' Leanne accused, choosing to emphasise her point by balling a fist and aiming it at his shoulder. A totally ineffectual gesture that reminded her of a butterfly senselessly batting its wings against a tiger.

'You possess an over-active imagination.'

He sounded amused, darn him, and she aimed a more forceful punch. 'Put me down, damn you!'

They reached her room, and he crossed to the bed and settled her carefully between the covers. 'I'll fetch the tablets in case you need them through the night.' Leanne closed her eyes against the sight of him, and prayed she might be asleep by the time he returned.

A hopeless appeal, for she was acutely aware of the moment he re-entered the room.

Her eyes flew open at the touch of his fingers as they brushed idly down her cheek.

'Sleep well,' he bade with teasing amusement, then he turned and left the room before she was able to summon a stinging response.

CHAPTER THREE

LEANNE woke feeling refreshed and without any lingering trace of a headache. Quickly tossing aside the sheet, she crossed to the large expanse of panelled glass and drew back the drapes.

It was a beautiful day, the sun bright, the sky clear of any clouds. Without pausing for thought she caught up a swimsuit and made for the *en suite*, emerging five minutes later to pull on shorts and a T-shirt before making her way down to the kitchen.

'Morning, Eleni.' She greeted the older woman who was busily occupied scouring a skillet at the sink.

An affectionate smile creased Eleni's features as she dried her hands and turned to give Leanne her undivided attention. 'Ah, how is the headache this morning?'

'Gone, thank goodness,' Leanne said with relief, and, crossing to the large refrigerator, she extracted fresh orange juice and filled a glass, then sipped from it with undisguised appreciation.

'Dimitri has already left for the city.'

Thank heavens for small mercies, Leanne said silently. Facing Dimitri at the start of her day would have been too much.

'He intends calling into the hospital this morning,' Eleni continued, relaying the message she'd been requested to convey. 'And he'll be home at six, so you can both go and visit Paige together.'

Her dark eyes filled with expressive warmth. 'The news you are to marry gives me much joy.'

It was on the tip of Leanne's tongue to take Eleni into her confidence and reveal that the engagement was a sham conceived entirely for Paige's benefit. Except that something held her back, and she accepted the housekeeper's affectionate hug with equal warmth.

'Thanks, Eleni.' It was difficult to look suitably starry-eyed, but she managed a credible smile.

'What can I get you for breakfast? Eggs? French toast?'

Eleni adored making a fuss, and Leanne's smile widened as she wrinkled her nose in silent negation. 'We play this game every time I come home,' she responded musingly. 'A banana, toast and coffee will be fine, and I'll get it after I've had a swim.'

It was almost ten when she slid behind the wheel of the Mercedes and drove to the hospital. Frequent short visits would prove less tiring for Paige, and Leanne divided up the day accordingly.

If anything, her mother seemed a little brighter, and, although pale, her features no longer looked quite so drawn.

'Darling, let me have a look at your ring,' Paige requested within minutes of Leanne's entering the suite, and Leanne dutifully extended her hand. 'It's simply beautiful, and a perfect fit.'

She managed a suitable rejoinder, and endeavoured to display a degree of fascinated pleasure in the diamond's multi-faceted brilliance.

Paige's eyes assumed a faint, dreamy expression. 'I saw the announcement in this morning's papers.'

Leanne hadn't thought to look. She'd spent ages in the pool, enjoyed a late breakfast, then rushed upstairs to shower and change.

'A small, private ceremony held at home next week,' her mother relayed wistfully. 'In the gardens. Isn't that wonderful?'

'Yes, wonderful.' What else could she do but agree?

'Have you decided what you'll choose to wear?'

'Not yet.' There was a rack of gowns in her wardrobe, any one of which would be eminently suitable for an informal engagement party.

'Dimitri has already conferred with my doctor, and, with a nurse in attendance, there's no reason why I can't be at the house for a few hours. A wedding-gown is so special,' Paige enthused gently. 'You'll look stunning in white.'

Wedding. Who said anything about a *wedding*? The feeling of panic momentarily robbed the breath from Leanne's body. 'Paige——'

'I wish I was able to go shopping with you,' her mother continued wistfully. 'There's that lovely boutique in Toorak, and you must ring Vivienne. She'll put everything aside and give you her undivided attention.'

A sense of disbelief washed over Leanne's body, and she felt stunned... but not for long. A slow-burning anger ignited and began to flare, coursing through her veins until she was consumed with it.

'Paige,' Leanne began, making every effort to maintain control. 'Dimitri and I——'

'Have known each other for years. Ten in all.' Beautiful blue eyes glowed with the immensity of Paige's pleasure. 'This wedding will be so special.

I've longed for the day you get married, and I'm overjoyed that you're bringing the date forward for my benefit.' She lifted a hand and covered Leanne's fingers. 'I'm going to have Vivienne bring in some gowns so I can make a suitable selection for myself as mother of the bride.'

Dear God. What had begun as a harmless conspiracy was now raging out of control. The question was, *why*?

She had to remain calm. No matter how angry she felt, she couldn't allow Paige to suspect that things were not as they seemed.

'Has Dimitri been in to see you this morning?' she queried gently, and her mother gave a slight nod.

'Early, darling. On his way into the office.'

Dimitri was incapable of being manipulated, not even by the circumstances of Paige's illness. Which meant he had to be a willing participant.

It killed her to smile, but she managed a credible facsimile. 'I shall take him to task for breaking the news.' The chiding amusement in her voice masked the threat of intent. She planned to *slay* him. She also had to get out of Paige's suite before her animosity became visible.

'I'll leave you to rest for a while,' she said in a light voice. 'I have to ring Vivienne, and begin some serious shopping. I'll be back after lunch.' Leaning forward, she touched her lips against her mother's cheek, then swallowed quickly against the lump that rose in her throat as she glimpsed the faint misting of tears which was evident.

The moment she left the suite a cold, hard anger rose from within her, and by the time she reached the car she was so maddened it was a minor miracle that she reached the city without incident.

The Kostakidas corporation had offices on a high floor in an ultra-modern steel and glass tower that held the ultimate in executive furnishings.

It was years since Leanne had visited its revered portals, and she moved with calculated calm towards Reception, unnerved by the stylishly attired young woman whose hair, make-up and clothes would have done credit to a model straight out of *Vogue* magazine.

'Dimitri Kostakidas,' Leanne stated with quiet authority.

'Mr Kostakidas is in conference,' the receptionist relayed with polite regret. 'Do you have an appointment?'

Leanne's expression was equally polite. 'Perhaps you could inform Dimitri's secretary that his fiancée is waiting to see him?' She even took the faint sting from her words by proffering a slight smile. 'I'm sure he won't object to the interruption.'

The girl's professionalism was superb. 'Of course,' she acceded at once, and, picking up the receiver from its console, she relayed the information, listened attentively, then replaced the receiver. 'Annita will be out in a minute to escort you to Mr Kostakidas's private lounge.'

Almost immediately an immaculately attired woman emerged into the foyer, her classical features expressing just the right degree of friendliness.

'Miss Foorde? How nice to meet you. May I offer my congratulations?' Her smile appeared genuine, and Leanne managed an appropriate response. 'If you'd care to come with me?'

Dimitri's private lounge was sumptuous, with deep-seated armchairs in buttoned soft black leather, and strategically placed occasional tables. A double set of cabinets lined one wall and floor-to-ceiling glass provided a spectacular view of the city.

'Dimitri won't be long,' Annita informed her. 'Can I get you a drink? Coffee? Something cool? A light wine, perhaps?'

She'd like to pour boiling oil over his head, but that was purely wishful thinking! 'Iced water would be lovely.' At least it might cool her down, and she thanked her as the woman handed her a glass filled with ice-cubes and chilled water before taking her leave.

Five minutes passed, followed by another five, and Leanne began to ponder darkly whether Dimitri was genuinely unable to extricate himself or merely providing time for the dissipation of her anger.

Fat chance, she derided silently, unable to prevent the faint tensing of her body as the door opened and the object of her rage entered the room.

In a formal dark business suit he looked formidable. Invincible, indomitable, and infinitely dangerous to any unwary adversary.

'Leanne.' Dimitri's voice was deceptively bland. 'This is an unexpected pleasure.'

Her eyes flew to his, and their depths were alive with the fiery sparkle of restrained anger. An emotion which was so consuming, it obliterated any respect for caution.

'You know very well why I'm here,' she returned heatedly.

His dark, faintly amused gaze merely added ammunition, and she got to her feet, ready to launch into further battle.

'Shall we do lunch?' His voice was a calm drawl finely edged with humour, and her eyes resembled intense blue sapphires as they flashed wrathful fire.

'How can you stand there and calmly suggest *lunch*?' she flung with subdued anger.

One eyebrow rose slightly. 'Paige can surely be forgiven for displaying a degree of sentimentality. In the normal course of events a wedding follows the announcement of an engagement.'

'Precisely. Except the engagement isn't real, and there'll never be a wedding!' Leanne drew herself up to her full height and still felt diminished, for even though she was in four-inch heels he towered head and shoulders above her. 'You could easily have put a brake on her enthusiasm, offered a simple explanation without hurting her feelings. Why didn't you?'

Dimitri crossed to stand within touching distance, and his close proximity sent a shiver of acute sensation scudding down the length of her spine.

'Were you able to disenchant her?' he queried with dangerous silkiness.

'Don't insult my intelligence,' she flung with soft vehemence. She took a deep, calming breath, then launched into scathing attack. 'No one, not even Paige, could manoeuvre you into any situation you found intolerable.'

His faint smile held a wry cynicism that was reflected in the darkness of his eyes. 'Is the idea of marriage to me so unacceptable?'

The weight of his words penetrated her brain, and she looked at him aghast. 'What are you trying to say?' she whispered.

'We've known each other for years, we share a mutual affection, and have no false illusions that the other is marrying solely for the acquisition of sizeable individual assets.'

Her eyes widened in shocked disbelief. 'That's crazy,' she uttered huskily.

'Is it?' Dimitri probed cynically, his gaze startlingly direct. 'There isn't an eligible woman of my acquaintance who wouldn't run far and fast if my fortune suffered a drastic reversal.' His lips formed a twisted smile. 'An honest arrangement is infinitely preferable.'

Take a deep breath, an inner voice urged, and try to retain hold of your sanity. 'I don't believe this.' Desperation clouded her vision, a desperation so real it almost tore the breath from her throat. 'What about what I want from life?'

He lifted a hand and caught hold of her chin, tilting it so that she had to look at him. 'Happiness, the security of a man you can trust at your side. Aren't those important qualities?'

Standing so close to him made her conscious of an elevated nervous tension, together with an electric awareness that was terrifying, and she held his gaze with difficulty. 'What about *love*?'

He was silent for several long seconds, then he ventured silkily, 'How do you define love, Leanne?'

As the most finite emotion between two people so acutely physically and mentally attuned to each other that it surpasses all else, she thought.

'I know what I want it to be,' she responded quietly, and his mouth curved to form a faintly wry smile.

'Idealism versus reality?'

'I haven't yet acquired your level of cynicism.'

'I would be disappointed if you had.'

She felt her stomach execute a few painful somersaults at the implications of such a marriage. Did she possess the courage to go through with it? *Dared* she?

'It would be positively *indecent* to arrange a wedding one week after the engagement announcement,' she ventured slowly. 'What would people think, for God's sake?'

'Either that you were holding out for marriage before allowing me into your bed,' he proffered lazily, 'or we'd been careless with contraception and you were carrying our child.'

She was powerless to prevent the faint tinge of pink that rose to her cheeks, and she only just prevented herself from throwing her glass at him.

'Do you doubt my ability to pleasure you in bed?'

Delicate colour sufused her cheeks, and she almost died at the degree of indolent humour evident in the gleaming eyes so close to her own.

Every single instinct screamed for her to wrench out of his grasp, to insist *now* that she fully intended to denounce any plans for marriage and acquaint Paige with the truth.

Yet she was held captive by the degree of sexual chemistry that was apparent between them, the intrusive weaving of a sensual magic so intense that it was all she could do to resist the instinct to sway towards him and invite his kiss.

Inner resolve was responsible for the gathering of courage needed to adopt a suitable response, and she forced her mouth into a musing smile and allowed a gleam of humour to lighten her eyes.

'I'm sure you possess the requisite finesse...' she said with teasing mockery, allowing words to slip from her tongue without conscious thought. 'If not, I can enlighten you as to my...' she paused imperceptibly '...preferences.' She deliberately raised one eyebrow and cast a seemingly careless glance round the room. 'I'm sure you could guarantee total privacy, but there's always the risk of interruption.' It took all her courage to continue, and she managed to inject a degree of teasing indulgence into her tone. 'Annita might be shocked if she caught her exalted boss and his fiancée immersed in the enjoyment of sex. Or worse.' She attempted a bewitching smile that held the temptation of Eve. 'I much prefer the bedroom, don't you?'

Dear God, what was she thinking of? It must be a form of divine madness to proffer such provocation, especially when she had absolutely no intention of following through.

'Privacy and comfort are a definite advantage,' Dimitri concurred with dangerous indolence, and she focused her attention on a point just behind his left ear.

Maybe if he thought she'd had several sexual encounters he wouldn't be so keen to go through with the wedding. A prospective husband could understand a long-lasting relationship, even more than one, given reasonable circumstances. But somehow she doubted that Dimitri would easily forgive promiscuity. Perhaps if she alluded to an active sex life, he'd be only too willing to agree to an annulment . . .

'I'll take you to lunch.'

Leanne's eyes flew to his, and she glimpsed the dark unfathomableness in his faintly hooded gaze.

'No,' she refused with a quick smile. The thought of sitting opposite him in a restaurant attempting to sip wine and fork food into her mouth would be more than she could bear. 'I promised Paige I'd be back at the hospital this afternoon, and I managed to get a hair appointment at five.' The latter was a fabrication, but she'd make a series of phone calls until she found a salon that would take her at that time. 'It will be easier for me to meet you at the hospital just after six.' All she wanted to do was get away from him, and she relaxed visibly as he turned towards the door.

'In that case, I'll walk you out to the lift.'

'I'm sure I can find my way.' Even to her own ears her voice sounded stiff, and she suffered his light clasp on her elbow and tried not to show her impatience as they passed through Reception.

Much to her relief, a lift arrived within seconds of pressing the call button, and she moved swiftly into the cubicle, infinitely glad when the doors closed and the lift began its electronic descent to the basement car park.

With the movements of an automaton she slid in behind the wheel and drove to Toorak where she successfully charmed Paige's hairdresser into giving her a late afternoon appointment. It was almost one, and she moved quickly towards the exclusive boutique Paige favoured. Even a few sample swatches would suffice, and perhaps a bridal magazine or two—anything to appease her mother's interest and divert her attention for an hour. Fortunately Vivienne had already been alerted, and there were numerous designs assembled from which to choose.

Paige had set her heart on Leanne wearing a full-length dreamy creation in silk and lace with a tiered veil, and a bouquet of cream orchids. The fact that Vivienne was in full agreement was a bonus, her expertise proving invaluable as she suggested, advised, and enthusiastically planned turning what Leanne had envisaged as a very small, intimate wedding into the social event of the year.

'Attending *numbers*,' the vendeuse dismissed, 'mean nothing. The Kostakidas name is sufficient to ensure that photos will appear in several newspapers and at least one of the country's leading magazines. Dimitri will doubtless forgo any camera crew in favour of a personal photographer, releasing one, maybe two photographs.' A bright, lacquered nail jabbed the open page of a glossy bridal magazine with fervour. 'So, everything will co-ordinate perfectly. We understand each other, *oui*?'

It was after three when Leanne entered the hospital, and she and Paige were chatting happily when Dimitri entered the suite some ten minutes later.

Leanne's pulse leapt at the sight of him, and for one brief second her eyes locked with his, only to skate to a point somewhere in the vicinity of his left shoulder.

The following thirty minutes became the longest half-hour in her life as she conversed with ease, although afterwards she had little recollection of a word she'd uttered. Once, she chanced a glance in his direction and glimpsed a tinge of humour apparent in those dark, gleaming depths, and thereafter she studiously avoided meeting his gaze.

After half an hour Paige began to visibly tire, and Dimitri got to his feet in one fluid movement, indicating that they would leave her to rest.

Minutes later they cleared Reception and walked out to the car park where his Jaguar was parked next to Paige's Mercedes.

'Are you going straight home?'

His drawled query provided the impetus for her to be contrary, and she summoned a seemingly regretful smile as she slid her key into the lock.

'No. I still have a few things to do before the shops close.' She opened the door and slid in behind the wheel, dismayed to see how he stood indolently at ease between the open door, one arm propped against the roof as he leaned down towards her.

'Eleni has prepared a celebratory dinner.' The thought of dining at home *à deux* caused a pang of dismay, and she cast him a speaking glance as she activated the ignition and fired the engine, feeling infinitely relieved as he straightened and closed the door.

She reversed with ease, and as she drove off she saw him get into his car, aware as she paused to enter the flow of traffic that the Jaguar was right behind her.

Dammit, where could she go for two hours? What she wanted to do was go home, change into a swimsuit and lounge round the pool with a long, cool drink. And something to eat. Which reminded her that she hadn't eaten a thing since breakfast.

The city didn't hold any appeal, so she simply headed towards Toorak, found a parking space, then popped in briefly to see Vivienne. Afterwards, she collected a few magazines and wandered into a trendy café where she ordered a salad sandwich, iced water and a cappuccino.

She needed time to relax, and it was easy to sit quietly and leaf leisurely through the magazine pages for half an hour. The wisdom of lingering any longer on her own didn't seem prudent when it became obvious that her solitary presence had been noted and speculated upon by two young men who seemed intent to test their macho appeal at any second.

There was an exquisite lingerie boutique within walking distance, and she browsed there contentedly, choosing to purchase a cream silk nightshirt and a few essentials before enduring an unnecessary shampoo and fractional trim—opting to have the length caught into an elaborate knot atop her head, rather than flowing freely about her shoulders.

At least the style was cool, and she emerged from the salon at six, aware with every kilometre she travelled that it was bringing her closer to the hospital—and Dimitri.

The Jaguar was conspicuous by its absence in the hospital car park, and Leanne breathed a faint sigh of relief as she locked the Mercedes.

Reception was quiet, and she made her way swiftly down the corridor to Paige's suite, only to come to an abrupt halt at the sight of Dimitri sitting at ease on the edge of her mother's bed.

He stood as she entered, and his smile held musing warmth, although his eyes were dark and unfathomable. 'I had George drop me,' he enlightened her evenly as Leanne quickly masked her surprise.

She moved forward to greet her mother, then she sank into the chair Dimitri pulled forward. He, much to her chagrin, chose to stand behind her, and she was consciously aware of the faint, elusive tones of his aftershave mingling with the clean smell of his clothing.

Every now and again she felt his hands settle briefly on her shoulders, and each time her heartbeat raced into overdrive. The ensuing hour became a parody as she attempted to inject her voice with enthusiasm and display the expected interest in arrangements for her impending marriage.

'Mid-afternoon, one week from today,' Dimitri revealed. 'I've arranged the celebrant, caterers, flowers, and invitations for a handful of guests.'

Dear God, it was like riding a roller-coaster that wouldn't stop.

'A weekend at one of the inner-city hotels will have to suffice in lieu of a honeymoon,' he continued with regret.

They both knew it was merely an excuse based on the acute precariousness of Paige's health, but Paige pretended otherwise.

'You must go to Greece,' she enthused, her eyes misty with remembered pleasure. 'The islands are so beautiful. Santorini. Rhodes.'

'We will,' Dimitri assured her gently. 'I promise.' He leaned forward and brushed his lips against her temple. 'You're tired. We'll leave you to rest, hmm?'

Leanne followed his actions, then walked at his side to the car, handed him the keys, and slid into the passenger seat.

The distance between hospital and home had never seemed so short, and with each passing kilometre she found it impossible not to feel as if a trap was steadily closing around her vulnerable neck.

The Mercedes slowed before the impressive set of gates, then traversed the drive and slid to a halt inside the garage.

'A drink before dinner?'

Leanne registered the drawled query as they entered the house, and she paused in silent contemplation. She'd barely eaten anything at breakfast and only a sandwich since ... Wisdom cautioned that alcohol in any form on an empty stomach was the height of folly. However, a small measure might give her the necessary courage to sit through a few courses of Eleni's gourmet offerings.

'Yes.' Decisiveness had to be an advantage, she considered as she preceded him into the lounge. 'A light white wine.'

Minutes later she sipped the cool, fresh chardonnay with appreciation, enjoying the faint warmth stealing invasively through her veins as it soothed a degree of elevated nervous tension.

'Is there anything you'd like to discuss?' she ventured lightly, and bore his slow, raking appraisal with equanimity for several minutes before fixing her attention in the vicinity of his right shoulder.

'Are you suggesting we indulge in the art of polite conversation?'

The drawled query held an element of humour, and she effected a slight shrug. 'Why not?'

'I gather anything is applicable,' he responded in vaguely cynical tones, the edge of his mouth lifting in quizzical speculation, 'as long as it doesn't touch on the wedding.'

Her stomach lurched, and decided not to settle too comfortably. Or maybe it was the effects of the wine.

'Or my ability to provide you with sexual pleasure,' he elaborated hatefully. 'As a matter of interest, how do you intend to measure my——?' he paused deliberately, then added with dangerous softness, 'Performance.'

Sheer bravado was responsible for her taking time to reply. That, and the need to shock. 'I've tried it, and found the experience to be vastly overrated.'

She had, once. With someone of whom she'd become very fond. And it had been a disaster. Simply because when the moment had arrived she'd panicked and called a halt before anything happened. Exit one very angry young man whose blistered riposte had rung in her ears for weeks. However, she had no intention of enlightening Dimitri of that fact.

'Indeed?' His voice sounded like velvet being shaved by the finest tensile steel blade. 'Perhaps I'll be able to change your opinion.'

Leanne pretended to accord him due consideration, her gaze dark and speculatively thoughtful. 'Perhaps,' she allowed with a faint shrug, aware that she was playing a dangerous game, and an extremely foolish one. 'Although you don't really turn me on.' She had to be mad, *insane*. Indulging in verbal foreplay with a man of Dimitri's calibre held all the potential dangers of an amateur juggling nitro-glycerine.

'Shall we go in to dinner?' Was that her voice? She sounded so calm, when inside she was quaking from an excess of nervous tension.

'Eleni has prepared your favourite moussaka,' he told her smoothly. 'She'll be upset if it begins to spoil.'

It took only one glance at the elegantly appointed table for Leanne to realise that the kindly housekeeper had utilised the finest damask, set out the best china, silver and crystal, and offset it all with elegant candles and flowers. A bottle of Cristal champagne rested to one side in a silver ice-bucket, and a single red rose lay diagonally beside each plate.

To one side lay a number of covered serving dishes, and Leanne was touched at the effort Eleni had employed to make this a special meal. It also made her feel like a traitor, for she knew Eleni's heart would be crushed should the truth of her alliance with Dimitri ever be revealed.

'Only a small portion,' she cautioned as Dimitri took her plate and prepared to serve the food.

As well as moussaka, there were parcels of minced lamb spiced with herbs and wrapped in vine leaves, delicious home-baked bread and thin slivers of veal dipped in egg and breadcrumbs and fried on a high heat that ensured a crisp coating on the tender meat. Delicate Greek pastries vied with a selection of grapes and cheeses to follow.

The food was delicious, Leanne knew, for Eleni possessed an enviable culinary flair. However, after the initial few mouthfuls she merely reassembled the contents of her plate, refused anything from the main selection, and just nibbled at a pastry before choosing a few grapes.

'Your appetite seems to have diminished to a point where it's almost non-existent,' Dimitri commented, and she effected a dismissive shrug.

'I didn't have lunch until late.'

'More champagne?'

Dared she? Somehow she didn't think so. 'No, thanks.'

They had maintained a discourse throughout the meal...polite *divertissements* that covered the state of the nation, the Kostakidas empire and the travels of its illustrious director. Sydney, Rome, Athens, Zurich, Lucerne and London within seven months was an impressive record.

Dimitri sat with ease, yet there was an inherent quality apparent, a primal essence that was wholly primitive. Intermingled with a devastating sexual alchemy, it proved a fearsome combination from which any sensible female would run and hide.

As the minutes ticked slowly by she began to feel stifled, supremely conscious of every pulsebeat, every single breath she took.

'I'll take everything through to the kitchen and put away the food.' It was the least she could do, and besides, Eleni would have retired to the flat she shared with George above the triple garage at the rear of the grounds. 'Then I'll make coffee.'

'I need to make an international phone call and send a few faxes,' he declared, unperturbed as he rose to his feet. 'Perhaps you wouldn't mind bringing my coffee into the study?'

She managed a negligent, monosyllabic reply, then systematically began placing everything on to the trolley before wheeling it through to the kitchen where she transferred food into the refrigerator before loading the dishwasher.

Ten minutes later the coffee was ready, and she poured some into a cup, filled a Thermos flask, then put both, together with cream and sugar, on to a tray before taking it to the study. It was a pleasant chore that she'd delighted in performing for Yanis on numerous occasions in the past, and the small table adjacent to the study door still remained, allowing her to set down the tray as she knocked before opening the door.

Dimitri was leaning against the side of the large rosewood desk, the telephone receiver held in one hand as he conducted a conversation in Greek to someone on the other end of the line.

Leanne's eyes flew to his tall, muscular frame, registering that he'd discarded his jacket, removed his tie, and loosened the top few buttons of his shirt.

With a hand thrust into his trouser pocket he exuded an aura of power that she found vaguely frightening, and she felt her stomach lurch, then contract with apprehension as she met his faintly hooded gaze.

She had no wish to eavesdrop on his conversation, despite being unable to comprehend so much as a word, and she moved silently to the desk, deposited the tray, then turned to leave, only to come to a halt as he caught hold of her wrist, successfully preventing her flight.

She looked at him in startled surprise, then opened her mouth to voice a silent protest, closing it again as he concluded his conversation and replaced the receiver.

His eyes were darkly inscrutable, and he cast the tray a quick glance, then raised an eyebrow in silent query at the single cup. 'You're not joining me?'

'No. It's too strong for my taste.' She made a controlled effort to keep her voice calm. 'Besides, I don't want to disturb you.'

All she wanted to do was run upstairs to her room, and she pondered the wisdom of inventing a headache—anything as a logical reason for escape.

'That's an interesting phrase,' he drawled as he stood up. He lifted a hand to her throat, then slid his fingers to cup her nape, impelling her forward.

She lifted both hands to his chest in an instinctive movement to prevent further contact, although the gesture proved fruitless as he curved an arm down her spine and pulled her close against him.

He was going to kiss her. She could see the gleam of intent mirrored in the depths of his eyes as his head lowered to hers.

She wanted to cry out, but no words emerged as his mouth closed over hers and began caressing with erotic slowness, his tongue a provocative instrument as it slid over her lips, then dipped into the moist cavern to tease and tantalise at will, demanding a response she found difficult not to give.

It was like being cast adrift in an unknown sea, and she felt terribly afraid, for there was a very real danger that she'd never make it to shore.

He wasn't playing fair, for his touch had undergone a subtle change as he created havoc with her senses and tipped her over the edge beyond rational control.

At her soft intake of breath his mouth hardened, taking possession with such innate mastery, she felt as if he was plundering her very soul.

All her senses were acutely attuned to this one man, and she felt achingly alive, her response generous and unbidden as he transported her to a place she had hitherto only visited in a host of wayward dreams.

A subtle shift in his hold as he pulled her close into the cradle of his hips made her shockingly aware of his swollen arousal, and she began to struggle, frightened of his strength and her own vulnerability.

Attempting leverage against his chest, she wrenched her mouth away from his . . . succeeding, she realised shakily, only because he chose to allow her to.

Dear lord in heaven, what had her foolish parrying invited? She wanted to turn and run, yet her limbs seemed frozen into immobility, and her eyes were wide and unblinking, their dark blue depths dilated to their fullest extent as she met his narrowed gaze.

His hands slid down her arms and curved against her ribcage, his thumbs brushing against the sides of her breasts, witnessing her instant reaction to his touch, the sweet burgeoning and sudden tightness of each vulnerable peak as he conducted an agonisingly slow, exploratory sweep that seemed to reach deep inside her, activating her sensual core until it flared and radiated through every nerve cell, every fibre, until she felt on fire.

It was damning, damnable, and there was nothing she could do to hide her response. Her mouth trembled, and she stood perfectly still as he lifted a hand and brushed his fingers across her softly bruised lips.

'I think we can dispense with any doubt that I fail to turn you on,' Dimitri taunted gently. His hand slid to her hair as he tucked a stray tendril back behind one ear. 'Go to bed.' He caught hold of her chin between thumb and forefinger, tilting it so that she had to look at him. 'And sleep—if you can,' he added softly.

She needed no second invitation, and only innate pride prevented her fleeing from the room and the inimical man who occupied it.

Instead, she forced herself to turn and walk slowly to the door, then closed it quietly behind her before making her way upstairs to her suite where she undressed, put away her clothes, removed her make-up, then slipped on a cotton nightshirt and slid in to bed to stare sightlessly at the darkened ceiling until sleep finally provided a blissful oblivion.

CHAPTER FOUR

THE days leading up to the wedding passed in a blur of activity as Leanne slotted fittings and shopping in between visits to Paige in hospital. Then there was the essential liaising with Eleni and the caterers, the numerous phone calls. Not to mention the necessity of taking a hurried flight to the Gold Coast in order to ensure that the manager to whom she'd entrusted the beauty clinic was prepared to continue on a more permanent basis, to arrange for the leasing of her apartment, the storage of her treasured belongings, and, lastly, to collect more of her clothes.

When she got back to Melbourne Dimitri, whether by circumstance or design, appeared equally busy, for he left the house before Leanne emerged downstairs for breakfast, and returned in time to visit Paige. Two evenings out of the ensuing four he claimed a prior dinner engagement with business associates, and returned long after Leanne had retired for the night.

She tried to tell herself that she couldn't care less, that she didn't want his attention—or his extended affection.

Yet deep inside she knew she lied. With each passing day she became more acutely sensitive to his every glance and move. And he knew, damn him. He was a master at any game he chose to play. While she was a mere novice in several. The knowledge was evident in the faint gleam of his eye, the slightly twisted smile, and it irked her unbearably.

Friday dawned bright and clear, and Leanne became swept along on a swift-moving tide that saw the arrival of numerous people, each engaged for a specific task.

By noon the marquee, which had been erected the day before, was filled with its complement of tables, each of which had been set with linen, cutlery and crystal, and decorated with orchids. The caterers arrived and took care of the food beneath Eleni's eagle-eyed supervision.

At one o'clock Leanne escaped upstairs to shower and change, while Dimitri drove to the hospital to collect Paige and an accompanying nurse.

Vivienne arrived at two—ostensibly to help Paige dress, and to assist Leanne with her gown and veil. Forty-five minutes later the photographer descended, closely followed by the celebrant.

Paige looked incredibly frail, yet there was an inherent strength apparent, almost as if she'd marshalled all her reserves together in order to make it through the next few hours.

It was perhaps as well that there was no time in which to think. If there had been, Leanne was sure she'd never have had the courage to go through with it.

Instead, she found herself walking at Dimitri's side towards the flower-festooned gazebo at the edge of the gardens, aware of Paige seated in a wheel-chair, and the celebrant's voice intoning a meaningful but brief ceremony legalising an alliance between Leanne Paige Foorde and Dimitri Yanis Kostakidas.

Wedding-rings were exchanged, and the groom kissed the bride.

There were more photographs, then champagne was served to the select collection of guests, followed by hors-d'oeuvres and more champagne.

The food was served at five-thirty, an epicurean delight featuring several European dishes to tempt the most discerning palate.

There were forty guests in all, and the only reason Leanne knew the number was because she asked Eleni. Most were people she knew, a few very well, others were business associates of Yanis and Dimitri, together with a handful of Paige's dearest friends.

At eight o'clock the guests, by prior arrangement, began to disperse, and when they had all gone Leanne slipped indoors to change out of her wedding-gown.

George had already stowed her bag, together with Dimitri's, in the boot of the Jaguar, and it was almost nine when Dimitri drew the car to a halt outside the hospital's main entrance.

Paige looked tired, her skin almost ashen and alarmingly translucent. But her eyes were alive, as bright and deep a blue as those of her daughter.

'We'll stay and see you settled,' Leanne declared gently, but Paige shook her head.

'No. I insist. Besides, I'm very tired.' Her smile was quite beautiful. 'Come and see me tomorrow. In the afternoon.' There was even a tinge of humour apparent in her voice. 'Not before.'

Leanne looked on helplessly as Dimitri lifted Paige from the car and placed her into the wheelchair, and there was only time for the briefest of affectionate hugs before a team of nurses converged and wheeled Paige out of sight.

She wanted to go home, to her own room, and forget the day's madness and all it entailed. Except that that wasn't possible.

For the past hour she'd felt akin to a dove held in the claws of a marauding hawk, heart fluttering almost out of control while she waited for the moment when he would strike and slash her delicate flesh to ribbons.

Leanne turned and walked back to the car, slipping into the passenger seat as Dimitri slid in behind the wheel.

'Would you like to go on to a nightclub?'

Images flickered through her mind of a dimly lit room, hazy with the pall of cigarette smoke and loud with the sound of music. There was always the chance that they might encounter Shanna if he chose one of the exclusive clubs he was known to favour on occasion, and somehow the thought of having to enact the part of an enraptured bride was more than she could bear. But the alternative of being alone with him in a hotel suite wasn't exactltty preferable, either.

Leanne shook her head in silent negation, then added a quiet refusal.

'Or somewhere for coffee?'

More than anything she wanted to slip out of her dress, remove her make-up, curl into a comfortable bed and go to sleep.

'No, thank you,' she declined with the utmost politeness. Leaning her head back against the cushioned head-rest, she simply closed her eyes as he fired the engine and sent the car purring smoothly out on to the street.

Ten minutes later the vehicle drew into the entrance of a stylish hotel, the concierge emerged to greet them and their bags were extracted while Dimitri took care of the registration.

Their suite was on a floor high above the city, large, luxurious, with appointments that put it in a class all of its own.

The porter deposited their bags, then retreated soundlessly after providing the usual spiel regarding the hotel's amenities.

The almost silent click of the door seemed unnecessarily loud, and Leanne cast a cursory glance round the room before allowing her attention to focus briefly on the kingsize bed.

Dear God, the days when a bride swooned with fear on her wedding night belonged in the Dark Ages. Yet the circumstances were far from typical; so, too, was the man she'd pledged to love and honour.

'There's champagne in the bar-fridge,' Dimitri drawled as he slid open his bag and began transferring clothes into the wardrobe.

Champagne? 'Why not?' she replied with an ineffectual shrug. It might also dispense with some of her nervous tension.

He crossed to the bar, extracted and opened the champagne, then handed her a slim flute.

Dammit, this room, the *bed*, was stifling her. Not to mention the man who seemed to dominate it. Maybe refusing to visit a nightclub hadn't been such a good idea, after all.

'We should have gone back to the house,' Leanne ventured, and incurred his faintly musing glance.

'Why destroy the illusion?'

'Paige——'

'The hospital have this number, and that of my mobile.'

There was nothing she could do to prevent the haunted look that crept into her eyes, and she took several sips of champagne in a desperate bid to gain some measure of control.

'I'll unpack,' she managed with outward calm, and, placing the flute down on to a nearby table, she crossed to her bag and began removing clothes, placing them on hangers, in drawer space; then, collecting toiletries and nightwear, she made for the adjoining bathrom.

She felt as tense as a tightly coiled spring, and without further thought she stripped off her clothes and stepped into the shower stall.

Warm water cascaded over her shoulders and down her back, and for several minutes she simply stood there, taking solace from the therapeutic fall of water, then she reached for the soap and worked a good lather before rinsing off.

Towelled dry, her toilet complete, she gathered up a nightshirt and slipped it on. The silk whispered over her curves, its hem coming to rest at mid-thigh. It wasn't exactly the ultimate in feminine appeal, she decided as she cast her reflected image a quick glance. However, she was damned if she'd don a filmy nightgown in deference to her role as a blushing bride.

Her hair was still piled on top of her head, and her fingers went automatically to the confining pins, loosening and discarding them before dragging her fingers through its length.

A pale-faced *child* with solemn eyes much too large for her delicate face stared back at her. Dammit, she looked about seventeen!

Years of fantasising about Dimitri in the role of lover was one thing. The reality was infinitely different.

Dear God, she'd never be able to go through with it—never, she despaired. Her hands curled round the vanity-unit surround, and her knuckles showed white as she attempted to gather together sufficient courage to move from the room.

Without giving herself time to think, she turned and emerged into the bedroom, coming to an abrupt halt at the sight of the large bed, its covers turned back, and the softened light of a single bedlamp. One glance in Dimitri's direction was sufficient to determine that he'd shrugged off his jacket, removed his tie, freed all the buttons on his shirt and pulled it free from his trousers.

He looked up and saw her, his gaze darkly inscrutable as he took in her cream silk nightshirt with its demure neckline and short sleeves. Then he moved towards the bathroom. 'I won't be long.'

Leanne lifted her shoulders in a negligible shrug. 'Take your time.' Take all night. In fact, take forever! she added silently.

Seconds later she heard the sound of the shower running, and she moved around the suite with the restlessness of a cat walking on hot bricks.

For one crazy moment she considered changing into her clothes and racing downstairs to call a cab, although that would achieve precisely nothing, except highlight her own insecurity and incur Dimitri's amusement.

Within minutes the shower stopped, and she closed her eyes tightly, then slowly opened them again. Tell him the truth, an inner voice urged. Sure, she argued silently. After all the provocative innuendo, would he believe her lack of experience?

A movement caught her eye and she turned slightly to see Dimitri enter the bedroom, his tall, muscular frame saved from complete nudity by the towel hitched carelessly at his waist.

He looked magnificent, broad shoulders, deeply tanned skin stretched over superb musculature, a deep, curling mat of dark hair covering his chest and arrowing down to a firm waist, and strong muscled thighs.

Leanne unconsciously caught her lower lip between her teeth, and tried to shrug off a feeling of helplessness as a tide of warmth swept through her body. Dammit, she'd seen him in less as he'd swum lengths of the pool. Why should the sight of a towel hitched round his hips cause such a stir?

Her heart stopped, then lurched into a runaway beat that visibly hammered at every pulse-point, and his eyes assumed a dark inscrutability as he watched the play of fleeting emotions chase across her expressive features.

Her stomach clenched with pain, knowing that he probably didn't care whether she slept with him or not. It angered her considerably that she would lose whether she chose to stay or retreat, for there was nothing to win.

Yet, as much as she wanted to turn and walk away, a perverse little imp inside her urged her to play the challenge to its bitter conclusion. For if she lay unresponsive in his arms the loss would not be entirely hers. A subtle form of revenge, but one that would be very sweet.

Her chin lifted, tilting at a proud angle as she held his gaze with unflinching regard. 'Shall we get this over with?' Did her voice sound as strangled to his ears as it did to her own?

One eyebrow rose in silent query. 'Wham, bam— thank you, ma'am?' he taunted silkily as he moved slowly towards her.

His raking scrutiny was daunting, and his eyes flared for an infinitesimal second, then became faintly hooded as he lifted both hands and framed her face.

His head lowered to hers, and his mouth savoured her soft, trembling lips before beginning a tantalising exploration of the delicate tissues within.

All her fine body hairs rose in self-defence against his deliberate eroticism, and she gave a silent groan of despair as liquid warmth began coursing through her veins.

She closed her eyes and willed her body not to respond, hating the way he was able to reach down to her soul and kindle desire with such infinite delicacy that it was all she could do not to lift her arms and wind them round his neck.

Warning flares activated her nerve-endings as his hands slid slowly down and slipped beneath the hem of her nightshirt to shape her buttocks, then slide over her hips to explore the soft concave of her waist, before trailing up to cup her breasts.

There was nothing she could do to prevent the slight aching fullness as each peak pulsated beneath his touch, or the involuntary catch of her breath as he eased the slither of silk from her body.

It took immeasurable courage to stand still while every instinct demanded an attempt at modesty, and her eyes assumed a haunting vulnerability as he gently brushed his fingers across each breast in turn before trailing down to the soft, curling hair at the apex of her thighs.

Without a word his head moved down to hers, and she gave a startled intake of breath as his mouth settled over the hollow at the edge of her neck and began teasing with such erotic sensitivity that she was powerless to still the degree of heightened emotion surging through her body.

It was like an encompassing heat that liquefied her bones and tore at the foundations of any inborn reserve, creating an ambivalence that was vaguely frightening.

She wanted to cry out as he curved an arm beneath her knees, and she felt incredibly helpless as he sank down on to the bed, his large frame seeming to loom much too close as he shifted towards her.

Slowly, with infinite ease, he lifted a hand and began tracing the soft contours of each breast, pausing to tease first one tender peak, then the other, before trailing low to probe with disturbing intimacy, his touch so electrifyingly provocative that it attacked the fragile tenure of her control.

Fire leapt through her body, and she arched away from him, gasping as she failed to escape his invasion, and her heart began to thud alarmingly as his lips settled in a vulnerable hollow at the base of her throat, teasing with sensual skill the rapidly beating pulse before grazing slowly down to the gentle swell of her breast to savour the soft tracery of veins.

Leanne cried out as he took the tightening peak into his mouth and began to suckle shamelessly, using the edge of his teeth to wreak an erotic havoc that trod a fine line between pleasure and pain.

His touch became a physical torment, and she was unaware of the soft, guttural sounds emerging from her throat as his mouth trailed slowly down to begin the most intimate exploration of all.

She lost the fragile hold on her sensual sanity and went up in flames, a willing supplicant to a driving hunger so intense that there was no room for shock, only a wild, pagan need that surpassed any restraint, and she reached for him, instinctively begging him to ease the throbbing ache deep within her.

Yet he was in no hurry to comply, and she moved restlessly beneath his touch as exquisite sensation spiralled through her body, consumed by such agonising sweetness that she began to sob in helpless despair.

Then he moved, his hard length a primitive invasion, and she gasped out loud as he began to withdraw, only to repeat the action several times, rendering such exquisite torture that she rose up and pressed her mouth against his shoulder, unaware of the tiny bites she rendered on his flesh until she tasted the salt of his blood.

With one slow movement he entered her, and she gave a faint whimper of distress as he stretched delicate tissues unaccustomed to accommodating such turgid rigidity.

Unbidden, her hands instinctively pushed against his shoulders in a desperate bid to be free of him.

'You sweet fool,' Dimitri growled in husky remonstrance. Taking extreme care not to move, he lowered his head and trailed his lips across her cheek, tracing a path to her mouth, his breath mingling with hers as she attempted to turn her face to one side.

'Don't,' she pleaded desperately, except that he wouldn't permit any such escape, and her muffled entreaty became lost as his mouth settled over hers, soothing, coaxing, so that she was unaware of the subtle movement of his body until it was too late. There was no pain, just the intense sensation of complete enclosure as she tightly encased him in warm, living silk.

He remained still for several timeless minutes, watching the softly fleeting emotions that chased across her expressive features as unused muscles flexed and contracted in an age-old rhythm that seemed almost beyond her control.

Leanne gasped as he began to move, his slow stroking so exciting that she clung to him as he urged her beyond mere pleasure to a state of sensual radiance so essentially pagan, it was all she could do not to cry out with the pleasure of sexual fulfilment.

Afterwards he brushed her mouth with his own in a light, tantalising caress that caused her lips to tremble in damnable reaction.

Slowly, with infinite care, he caught her close and rolled on to his back, carrying her with him so that she lay cradled against his chest. One hand captured her nape while the other trailed down to rest at the base of her spine.

She could feel the powerful beat of his heart so close to her own, and his skin smelt faintly musky. For some strange reason she wanted to edge out her tongue and taste it, and the desire to stretch like a contented feline was almost more than she could bear.

Leanne was conscious of every nerve-end, the faint ache of unused muscles, the slight tenderness of her breasts as they pressed against the mat of hair covering his chest, not to mention the highly sensitised tissues deep within her.

'You played a dangerous game, little cat,' Dimitri chided gently. 'A lover displays more finesse with an untutored innocent than he affords a partner well-versed in the art of lovemaking.' His fingers travelled slowly up her spine, then slid to frame her face, lifting it so that she had no option but to look at him.

The muted light lent his strong features various angles and planes, and his eyes were dark and slumberous. For the life of her she couldn't remove her gaze from his mouth. It fascinated her, the slightly fuller lower lip, the curved shaping that was infinitely sensual.

Remembering just how erotic his plunder had been of her body brought a slow suffusing of colour to her cheeks, and she lowered her lashes in an effort to hide the intensity of her emotions.

'Please let me go,' she said quietly, and she attempted to push herself away from him—without success, for his hold tightened measurably.

'You're uncomfortable?'

Not physically. However emotionally, mentally, she felt incredibly ill at ease. 'I must be heavy,' she protested hesitantly, and sensed his slow smile.

'You're a lightweight,' he drawled, then cautioned musingly, 'Continue moving like that, and I won't be answerable for the consequences.'

'You're still...' She trailed off, unable to find the right words, and she blushed as he finished huskily,

'In possession of you?'

She suddenly felt very young, and extremely inexperienced. '*Yes.*'

His soft chuckle was almost her undoing, but he shifted carefully, then curled her close to his side.

Her body ached, inside and out, and she made no protest as he slid from the bed. Seconds later she heard the sound of running water, and within minutes he returned and scooped her into his arms.

To feel so acutely shy seemed ridiculous, given the degree of intimacy they'd shared, yet there was an innate reserve that forbade any further loss of inhibitions as he placed her in the capacious spa-bath, then stepped in to sit beside her.

It was easy to close her eyes and let the bubbling water provide its soporific magic, and afterwards she stood silently quiescent as Dimitri towelled her dry before leading her back to bed.

'Dimitri——'

Anything further she might have uttered died in her throat as he tugged her down beside him, and on the edge of sleep the last thing she remembered was the possessive trail of his fingers across her skin, and the brush of his lips against her hair.

CHAPTER FIVE

LEANNE woke slowly, aware in those few seconds before total consciousness that something was different. The morning sun normally beat against the closed drapes from another direction, and she never slept nude.

Then she remembered.

Cautiously she turned her head, and discovered that she was alone. The rumpled sheets and tossed pillows were vivid reminders of how she'd spent the night and with whom.

And, as if that weren't sufficient, her body ached with the subtle evidence of Dimitri's invasion. She was extremely aware of her breasts, and their faintly tingling peaks. Sensitive tissues deep within her were still sensitive from his shameless possession as she'd followed an inherent instinct as ageless as Eve.

Even the mere thought of her response was enough to make a mockery of her intention to remain like ice in his arms.

Ice? She'd resembled a flame, consuming, generous, and blazing fiercely with desire.

Leanne closed her eyes against a host of chaotic memories, then opened them again.

Her eyes travelled to the electric clock on the nearby pedestal, and she gave a soft groan of despair, for it was well after eight.

'Breakfast?'

She raised her head at the sound of that drawled query, and pushed a shaky hand through the length of her hair. After last night, she really didn't want to face him at all.

Dimitri crossed to the bed and stood regarding her tousled appearance with musing indulgence. 'Orange juice, cereal, toast, coffee?'

Attired in jeans and a casual knit shirt, he looked indecently healthy, exuding a raw masculinity that was arresting and far too disruptive to her peace of mind.

'Start without me,' she said in a slightly husky voice, and felt infinitely relieved as he turned and retraced his steps to the table.

The tantalising aroma of bacon and eggs teased her nostrils, intermingling with strong, hot coffee. It made her realise just how hungry she was, and without hesitation she carefully draped the sheet around her and slid from the bed.

Collecting fresh underwear, she selected a slim-fitting cotton dress, then she moved to the *en suite*, emerging almost ten minutes later ready to face the day.

'I've already phoned the hospital,' Dimitri revealed as she took a seat opposite him at the table. 'Paige spent a reasonably comfortable night.'

Leanne managed a polite response, and concentrated on drinking her orange juice, then she opened the single-serving packet of cereal and poured it into the bowl, added milk, and began eating.

She was acutely aware of every movement she made, every breath she took in an effort to portray normalcy. Her entire body felt as if it was a tautly stretched wire, her emotions almost beyond any measure of control. It wasn't a feeling she was comfortable with, any more than she was comfortable with the man who aroused them.

'What would you like to do this morning?'

Leanne carefully replaced her cup down on to its saucer, and endeavoured to meet his gaze.

'We don't necessarily have to be together, if you have anything of importance...' She trailed off, her voice portraying extreme politeness.

His eyes narrowed fractionally. 'Now, why would you imagine I'd arrange anything more important this weekend than spending time with you?' he queried with deceptive softness.

It was crazy to feel so acutely fragile. 'Dimitri——' She foundered, wanting to scream out that she found it impossible to come to terms with the degree of intimacy they'd shared, or her own libidinous reaction.

'Don't hide from me,' he warned quietly, and, reaching out, he caught hold of her chin and tilted it fractionally so that she had to look at him. 'Or attempt to pretend we're not physically in tune with each other.'

'Damn you,' she cursed shakily, hating him. 'I'm not ready for that sort of honesty.'

'Perhaps not,' he drawled. 'But I won't allow you the illusion of psychological deception.'

'I'm going for a walk,' Leanne said tightly. 'I need some fresh air.'

'Finish your coffee,' he bade her easily, relinquishing her chin. 'We'll drive down to Frankston, have an early lunch, then visit Paige.'

She was mad to retaliate, insane to consider flouting him, but she was damned if she'd accept his direction with lamb-like docility. 'What if I'd prefer to stay in the city?'

'Do you foresee dragging me into various boutiques as some form of subtle revenge?' Dimitri countered, then he added musingly, 'Be warned, I'll insist you personally model every prospective purchase to my satisfaction.' His faint smile held humour at her expressive reaction. 'Changed your mind?'

She wanted to hurl something at him, and it irked her terribly that he knew. 'Frankston sounds good,' she managed sweetly, and, standing up, she retreated into the *en suite* to apply minimum make-up, then she collected her shoulder-bag and moved to the door.

The Jaguar was parked out front, the motor running, with the uniformed concierge standing in attendance, when they emerged from the main entrance. Leanne slid into the passenger seat while Dimitri walked round to slide in behind the wheel.

It was a beautiful day, the sun glorious in a cloud-free sky. Ideal for a scenic drive along the Mornington Peninsula.

The large car manoeuvred its way through inner-city traffic, then gathered speed as Dimitri gained the Nepean Highway.

Frankston was remarkably picturesque, with magnificent homes along the old Mornington Road area and Mount Eliza, the latter being a classy, trendy little community Leanne had visited with Paige on a few previous occasions.

Dimitri parked close to the sea, and they walked along the sandy foreshore. The salty tang smelled fresh and clean, and there was a soft breeze, warm from the summer heat, that teased the soft tendrils of Leanne's hair. Soft, pale sand lent a contrast to the blue bay sparkling beneath the sun's rays, and she felt an easing of inner tension as she walked silently at Dimitri's side.

There was a sense of togetherness that hadn't been in evidence for a long time... almost five years, she realised silently. For some strange reason she wanted to reach out and tuck her hand in his, to have him draw her close against him and raise her face to receive his kiss. To smile, and laugh a little, to share some of her innermost thoughts and question his.

Yet she did none of those things, and wondered why. Perhaps it was fear of rejection, fear that he would misconstrue her actions and place some sexual connotation on her innocent need for friendly companionship.

'Lunch?'

She paused by his side, and spared his arresting features a solemn glance. Then she smiled, her eyes blue and clear. 'Yes.' The sea air had renewed her appetite, and she felt the need for a long, cool drink.

He chose a small café that wasn't filled with weekend tourists, and ordered cold chicken with a delicious side-salad, and fresh fruit.

It was after two when they left, and almost three when they drew to a halt in the hospital car park.

Paige was asleep when they entered her suite, and in repose her features looked very pale, with a translucence that caused Leanne concern as she crossed to the bed and lightly touched her mother's shoulder.

Paige roused, and her eyes widened, then sparkled with pleasure as she eased into a more comfortable position.

'Leanne, Dimitri,' she greeted softly. 'Is it afternoon already?' Her gaze settled on her daughter in searching appraisal, as if seeking something indefinable, and Leanne wanted to cry out that love didn't come swiftly in the night, and sexual enlightenment was something else entirely.

'It was a beautiful wedding,' Paige voiced with a soft smile, and her eyes shone with remembered pleasure as they moved from Dimitri to her daughter. 'You looked wonderful, darling.' She turned towards her son-in-law. 'Didn't she?'

Dimitri reached out and caught hold of Leanne's hand, lifting it to his lips as he brushed her knuckles lightly. His eyes never left hers, and for a moment she thought she might drown in those dark depths. 'Beautiful,' he agreed gently.

Leanne couldn't breathe, and long seconds later she tore her gaze away from his, only to meet the small gleam of satisfaction in her mother's eyes.

Dear God, in a minute she'd choke, or blush. Or both.

'Now, what have you planned for the rest of the day?' Paige asked, and Dimitri smiled.

'A lazy afternoon. We drove down to Frankston this morning.' He leant forward and brushed his lips against her temple. 'We'll call in and see you before we go out to dinner.'

Leanne was silent in the car, and in their suite she moved quickly into the adjoining bathroom to change into a black maillot, over which she pulled a cotton T-shirt, then she gathered up a towel and a tube of sunscreen cream before emerging into the bedroom.

'I'm going for a swim,' she revealed, and glimpsed his lazy amusement as he looked up from reading from the day's newspaper.

'A desire for exercise, or a need for solitude?'

'*Both*,' she answered succinctly.

'Don't stay in the sun too long,' he warned softly.

Without a word she crossed to the door, opened it, then allowed it to close quietly behind her before moving towards the lifts.

It was a very luxurious hotel, and the swimming-pool was situated on the roof. A huge tiled affair with sparkling water, an abundance of sun-loungers, umbrellas, a small bar, and waiters in attendance.

There were also several people, which rather spoiled her quest for solitude. Although, to be honest, her reason for escape had been motivated by a need to be free of Dimitri's disturbing presence. At least for a while, she qualified darkly.

Possessed of a light tan, she smoothed in cream, slid her sunglasses in place, then lay face down on a full-length sun-lounger. Thirty minutes, then she'd change position, she promised herself as she closed her eyes and gave herself up to the relaxing warmth of the sun.

She must have dozed, for she came sharply awake at the touch of a hand against her shoulder, and she turned to see Dimitri stretched out on an ad-joining lounger.

Attired in black silk swimming-trunks he exuded dynamic masculinity, together with an inherent vitality that was infinitely dangerous to her peace of mind.

How long had he been there?

'You're turning pink,' he said indolently, and she turned over and lay on her back.

'I slathered on heaps of cream,' she defended, and she closed her eyes in the hope of ignoring his presence.

With little success. After five minutes she simply gave up trying and slid to her feet. Seconds later she executed a clean dive into the pool, and stroked several lengths before resting momentarily at the pool's edge, then she levered herself on to the ledge and caught up her towel, watching idly as Dimitri followed her actions.

He was a good swimmer, utilising strong, clean strokes in a natural rhythm that reminded Leanne of a sleek jungle beast. Then she shivered slightly, and blamed herself for possessing a fanciful imagination.

Towelled dry, she caught the length of her hair and wrung the excess water from it, then she wound the towel sarong-wise round her slender frame as Dimitri levered himself from the pool in one easy movement.

Minutes later they took the lift down to their suite.

'Can you be ready in an hour?'

Leanne spared him a quick glance. 'Of course. Do you want to take the shower first, or shall I?'

'We could take it together,' he suggested with cynical mockery, and her eyes assumed a brilliant blue.

'I don't think so,' she declared evenly, turning away from him, and his soft chuckle was nearly her undoing.

Leanne was ready at six, looking elegant in a black velvet evening dress with exquisite gold beading. Created by the acclaimed Australian designer, Daniel Lightfoot, it was strapless, its hemline resting fractionally above the knee, and came with a matching evening cape. Purchased after one of his recent showings on the Gold Coast, it moulded her slim curves and provided a startling contrast for her silver-blonde hair.

Dimitri was already waiting when she entered the lounge, and his eyes gleamed in silent appreciation, then dropped lazily to the full curve of her lips before slipping down to the gentle swell of her breasts.

A pale tinge of colour crept across her cheeks as sheer sensation unfurled deep within her and spread through her body like liquid fire. For one small second her expression betrayed a haunting vulnerability, then she tilted her head fractionally and summoned a faint smile.

'Shall we leave?'

Paige was tired, and appeared weaker in just the few hours since they'd seen her last. Leanne experienced a terrible sense of foreboding as they drove into the city. There were words she wanted to say, queries that required reassurance. But she kept silent, knowing there could be no reassurance.

She would have liked to go home. *Home*, not the hotel suite where they were booked into for another night. And she wanted to be alone with the infinite degree of sadness which filled her heart—for the wonderful woman who was not only her mother, but her friend. Most of all, she wanted to rage against fate for stealing away someone so good, so very kind, before her time.

The restaurant was exclusive, expensive, and offered excellent cuisine.

Leanne ordered soup *de jour*, followed by a seafood dish, and opted for fresh fruit instead of dessert.

Dimitri chose an excellent white wine, and she took a sip from her glass, then set it down. After last night she felt ill at ease in his company, and she launched into a discourse of inconsequential small-talk touching on a variety of subjects but focusing on none.

It was almost ten when he indicated that they should leave, and Leanne walked at his side to the car, choosing to sit in silence during the short drive to the hotel.

Inside their suite, he queried mildly, 'Coffee?'

Leanne didn't even hesitate. 'No. It keeps me awake, and I didn't——'

'Get much sleep last night?'

He sounded amused, damn him, and it rankled unbearably.

'You've consciously avoided eye contact with me for most of the evening,' Dimitri drawled. 'Why so shy?'

'Perhaps because I am!' Leanne retorted, then hated herself for taking the defensive.

'You found last night's experience...' He paused imperceptibly, then continued with musing cynicism, 'Overwhelming?'

Soft colour crept over her cheeks, and she clenched her hands in silent anger. 'I think you——' She faltered, then took a shallow breath and continued, 'Deliberately set out to shock me.'

One eyebrow rose slightly and his mouth edged to form a faintly mocking smile. 'Not to please you?'

That he'd succeeded was something she was unwilling to admit—even to herself.

Her eyes skittered away from his, all too aware of the latent gleam in those dark depths, the slight cynicism apparent there.

A shaft of pain speared through her body, and she met his gaze with difficulty. 'You have the unfair advantage of vast experience,' she said stiffly.

His eyes gleamed with latent mockery. 'A repeat of which you'd prefer to avoid—tonight.' His hand trailed to her nape, tilting her head so that the extent of her fragility was exposed.

'I really am tired.'

'Then go to bed,' he said gently.

'Alone?' Her eyes felt far too large, and she was unable to prevent the tip of her tongue from running over her lower lip in a purely nervous gesture.

'No,' he drawled, watching the fleeting tinge of colour shade her cheekbones.

Leanne was mesmerised by his dark, gleaming gaze, and haunted by the sensually curved mouth that descended slowly to capture hers in a light, erotic tasting—teasing, yet withholding the promise of passion.

Then he lifted his head, and she felt strangely bereft as he gently pushed her to arm's length.

For a moment she stood hesitantly, unsure, then without a word she turned and made for the bathroom where she discarded her clothes, removed her make-up, then slipped into a silk nightshirt.

When she emerged he was already in bed, and she slid quietly in between the sheets.

She lay still and closed her eyes, then gave a start when he reached out and snapped off the bedside light.

'Goodnight, Leanne.'

His faint amusement curled like a painless whip round her heart. Deceptively soft, yet infinitely possessive.

She was in no doubt that he'd instigated a deliberate play upon her emotions, and it hurt like hell that she'd allowed him to succeed.

Without a word she turned on to her side, only to give a startled gasp as firm hands clasped her waist and pulled her into the warm curve of his body.

His arm rested on her hip, and one hand settled possessively over her breast, shaping the softness with easy familiarity.

She felt his lips brush her hair, and settle briefly against her temple, and she closed her eyes.

'Don't,' she pleaded, certain that she'd never be able to remain immune. Unsure that she even wanted to.

With minimum effort he turned her towards him, and her hands instinctively moved to his shoulders when his mouth settled over her own in a gentle, teasing tasting that gradually assumed passionate intensity as he drank deeply from the moist, sweet cavern, taking as much as she was prepared to give.

It wasn't enough, Leanne decided hazily as she uttered a murmured protest when his mouth left hers and began a tortuously slow path to her breasts.

She was hardly aware of the gentle tug that dispensed with her nightshirt, and she gave a soft moan as he took possession of one tender peak.

An arrow of desire shot through her body, radiating until every pore, every sensitised nerve-end seemed to pulse with sensual life. It became all-encompassing, all-consuming, and negated any logical thought except the need for him to ease the ache deep within her.

She wasn't aware of the guttural pleas that escaped her lips, or the groan of despair as he trailed a tantalisingly slow path over her midriff, down the soft planes of her belly, to offer succour to the most intimate cavern of all.

Several long minutes later she gasped out loud as he began a merciless assault that almost tipped her over the edge, and she reached for him, her fingers heedlessly pulling his hair as she begged him to stop.

It was sheer torment, and she was almost demented when he lifted his head and began to explore one inner thigh, nipping the tender flesh when she dug her fingers into the hard sinew of his shoulders.

Then he moved, and she arched instinctively as he entered her, sliding slowly through the tight, silken tunnel that stretched sweetly to accommodate him.

This time there was no pain, only the erotic sensation of complete enclosure as she absorbed his throbbing length.

It felt so good, so *right*, and she was beyond caring as he encouraged her to match his movements, increasing the pace until they were in perfect unison.

The warm turbulence became a tumultuous rhythm that tossed her high, suffusing every nerve-end with electrifying passion as he led her towards a climactic orgasm so complete, it transcended every emotional plane and left her spent, consumed with such agonising sweetness that she didn't possess the will to move.

She was dreamily conscious of the drift of his fingers as they caressed the softness of her breasts, and the gentle touch of his lips against her own.

The last thing she remembered was the sheet settling across her shoulders, and the human warmth of arms enfolding her close as she fell asleep.

It was late morning when Leanne and Dimitri checked out of the hotel and drove back to the Toorak mansion.

Eleni had prepared a veritable feast for lunch, and, although Leanne attempted to do the food justice, her appetite was sadly lacking.

Perhaps it was a sense of premonition, for no sooner had they vacated the dining-room than Dimitri took a call from the hospital to say that Paige had taken a turn for the worse.

They arrived to discover that she'd been moved into the intensive-care unit and placed under heavy sedation.

There was nothing anyone could do, except be there as Paige slipped in and out of consciousness.

The vigil lasted another two long days and nights; a vigil they both shared in shifts until the early hours of Wednesday morning when Dimitri took Leanne home.

CHAPTER SIX

THE days following Paige's funeral slipped by, each a little less painful than the last as Leanne lost herself in completing innumerable tasks, and when there was none left she helped Eleni in the kitchen, conducted an unnecessary spring-clean, then diverted her attention to the gardens. Her actions were automatic, determined, and clearly indicative of a need to ease the grieving process.

There were times when it was all too easy to bring Paige's laughing features to mind, to visualise her smile and hear her lilting voice.

The memories they'd shared had been so very special, the bond between them closer than most. It was something she would treasure for the rest of her life.

Introspection began to intrude like a dark invader, and it seemed inevitable that Dimitri should become the central pivot of her existence, and their marriage.

With Paige's passing, there was no longer any need for pretence. Despite any resolution Leanne made, she was powerless to stop the acute sensations Dimitri was able to arouse, and she began to hate herself for the way she responded to the slide of his hand over her smooth skin, the touch of his mouth on her own.

Yet there was an inherent need to lose herself in his lovemaking, to become so caught up with the wild surge of emotions that she forgot everything except the magic of the moment. Afterwards she slept, only to wake and face the reality of each new day.

One morning, barely half an hour after Dimitri had left for the city, she simply collected her bag, informed Eleni that she'd be back by late afternoon, then entered the garage and slid in behind the wheel of the Mercedes.

It was a beautiful day, with only a few drifts of cloud in a pale blue sky. The sun was hot, and she automatically activated the car's air-conditioning unit.

With no idea of where she would go, she simply headed the car south and drove, instinctively choosing the Nepean Highway and the Mornington Peninsula.

The traffic was heavy until she cleared the outer suburbs, then it began to ease as she neared Frankston.

There were any number of beaches *en route* to Portsea at the furthest tip of the Peninsula, and Leanne eased the car to a halt on a grassy verge at the seaside town of Rosebud overlooking the expanse of Port Phillip Bay.

For what seemed an age she gazed out towards the horizon where the sea merged with the sky, lost in reflective thought.

Almost unaware of her actions, she slid from the car and locked it, then set out along the sandy foreshore.

A faint breeze tugged the hem of her skirt and teased the length of her hair as she walked. In the distance a few seagulls took to the air from their forage for food, circling low out over the water before gliding back to dig their long, curved beaks into the wet sand.

Every now and again the silence was broken by a keening gull, and after a while Leanne turned and began retracing her steps, surprised just how far she had come.

Inevitably her thoughts turned to Dimitri and their marriage...an alliance conceived from loyalty for a woman they had both adored.

A dangerous alliance, Leanne conceded, aware of the depth of her own emotions. She had little doubt that Dimitri viewed the marriage as a highly successful merger, for it tied several loose ends neatly together. His father's bequest to Paige was now within his control. He had a wife for whom he held affectionate regard; someone he could rely on to act as his social hostess.

But was it enough? Could she bear it when mere affection was no longer sufficient, and he began to seek attention elsewhere? With someone like Shanna?

A sudden chill whipped through her body, and she hugged her arms close to her midriff. If he should turn away from her, she knew she'd wither and die.

She had wealth and property worth millions. The ability to have almost anything she desired, and to travel anywhere in the world. Yet what she wanted was beyond price.

The crazy part was that she already had his name; she occupied his house and his bed. The question was, could she occupy his heart? Dared she even try?

She was mad, insane to want it all. The sensible thing to do would be to confront him, offer him a release from the marriage, and return to her former life on the Gold Coast.

At least, if she instigated such a proposal, it would be less hurtful than going with the status quo and discovering somewhere down the track that he'd taken a mistress.

It was after eleven when she gained the grassy verge and walked the few remaining steps to her car. With deft movements she unlocked the door and slid in behind the wheel, then reversed out and urged the vehicle towards town. It was too early for lunch, but she felt the need for a cool drink.

After exploring the township of Rosebud, she drove to Portsea, where she ate her usual salad sandwich in a little café before heading home.

'Dimitri rang,' Eleni informed her as she entered the kitchen. 'I am to remind you of the dinner tonight.'

'*Damn*.' The curse whispered from her lips as she recalled the worthy charity to which Paige had lent her support, and the fundraising function scheduled for this evening. A prestigious event held in the banquet-room of a select inner-city hotel, it was guaranteed to be attended by a number of wealthy patrons.

She vaguely recalled Dimitri mentioning that they were to assemble in the hotel lounge at six for drinks. Which meant she had precisely two and a half hours to search her wardrobe for something suitable to wear, shower, and tend to her nails, make-up and hair before they had to leave.

She managed it with five minutes to spare, looking coolly sophisticated in a stunning electric-blue silk gown with matching beaded jacket. The colour highlighted the clear texture of her skin, and gave emphasis to her silver-blonde hair, which she'd deliberately styled into a swirling knot atop her head. Jewellery was confined to a diamond pendant, matching earstuds, and a slim gold bracelet at her wrist.

Dimitri looked devastating in a black dinner-suit, white silk shirt and black tie. He possessed an animal grace that reminded her of a jungle predator... sleek, powerful, and infinitely dangerous.

'Ready?'

His musing drawl made all her fine body hairs stand up in protective self-defence. 'To enter the fray?' she countered solemnly, and incurred his level gaze.

'You don't want to go?'

Leanne drew a deep breath and released it slowly. 'I'm not looking forward to the inevitable scrutiny we'll receive.'

His eyes narrowed slightly as they swept her pale features. 'I think you're being overly sensitive.'

She gave a negligible shrug. 'Perhaps.'

'Paige gave a lot of her time and effort to this particular organisation,' Dimitri reminded her quietly, his gaze direct and vaguely analytical. 'I'm sure she would have wanted us to represent her tonight.'

Leanne was unable to suppress the faint quickening of her pulse at his nearness. He had the strangest effect on her equilibrium, making her aware of a primitive alchemy, a dramatic pull of the senses that was devastating.

She managed to hold his level gaze, and proffered a slight smile. 'Yes, I guess so.'

The drive into the city took longer than anticipated due to the heavy flow of traffic, and the sheer number of cars attempting to park provided inevitable delays. Consequently it was after six when they entered the huge formal lounge adjacent to the banquet-room.

Leanne stood quietly at Dimitri's side, greeting numerous acquaintances who paused to offer a mixture of congratulations and condolences.

Several waiters and waitresses circled with trays bearing glasses of champagne, orange juice and mineral water, and Dimitri followed her selection of the latter.

'Darlings, how *are* you?'

Leanne turned her head slightly at the sound of a familiar voice, and she was unable to suppress a winsome smile at the sight of a plump matron whose flowing, multi-layered attire and large-brimmed hat had become her trademark. She was also a committee member and generous benefactor whose tireless efforts had helped raise hundreds of thousands of dollars over the years, Paige had assured Leanne several years ago on just such an occasion as this one.

'Alethea,' Leanne greeted her with genuine pleasure.

'*Thrilled* to hear of the wedding. Devastated about poor, darling Paige.' She looked almost tearful, then she brightened considerably. 'A good crowd tonight. With luck, the children's hospital will acquire another mini-bus.' She reached out and patted Leanne's arm. 'You're a sweet girl.'

With surprisingly lithe movements she turned and moved through the groups of mingling guests.

It was an event which several people chose to patronise in an effort to be seen, Leanne mused as she allowed her gaze to wander idly, noting several well-known personalities, a few of whom wore sufficient jewellery to provide an insurance nightmare.

At seven the doors to the banquet-room opened and guests began to file in to take seats at their allotted tables.

'Who are we seated with?' Leanne asked as Dimitri took her elbow.

'Does it matter?'

Only the most insensitive planner would have placed Shanna at their table, and Leanne breathed a faint sigh of relief on her discovery that the tall brunette was nowhere in sight.

But her relief turned to dismay when the stunning model made a dramatic entrance halfway through the first course. Attired in a strapless, backless design in black velvet, she drew every eye in the large room as she *glided*, for want of a better description, Leanne mused silently, towards her designated table, several metres away.

Far enough away to preclude any immediate contact, Leanne observed with unaccustomed uncharitableness, but close enough to be reasonably accessible once the meal was concluded and the tables were cleared.

Leanne finished her starter, then did justice to the delicately stuffed breast of chicken with accompanying vegetables, and she declined dessert, refused to be tempted by the cheeseboard, and opted for a slim flute of champagne as opposed to mineral water in the hope that it would soothe a growing sense of unease.

Entertainment for the evening was a thirty-minute fashion parade by both male and female models featuring garments by Australian designers, after which the catwalk was dismantled while coffee was served to enable those who chose to dance to take the floor.

It signalled an opportunity for friends to move from one table to another, and Leanne wondered just how long it would be before Shanna opted to grace them with her presence.

'Dimitri. *Leanne*'

The smile was bright, too bright, as the beautiful brunette slid into a vacant seat next to Dimitri, and Leanne matched it with a diluted version of her own, aware that her actions were the subject of veiled conjecture by several guests.

'Shanna,' she responded with friendly politeness, while inwardly damning the man at her side for the seemingly warm greeting he extended.

How did one cope in the presence of a husband's former mistress? Leanne agonised, hating the hard knot of pain in the region of her heart.

With considerable aplomb, innate good manners, and an excellent attempt at acting, an inner voice told her.

'Poor Leanne,' Shanna purred with feigned sympathy as she lifted a hand and let her fingers rest lightly against Dimitri's arm. 'You must be *lost* without Paige.'

Steady, Leanne counselled herself silently. Just go with the flow. 'As well as being my mother, she was my best friend,' she offered with quiet honesty, and glimpsed the faint glimmer of envy in the model's beautiful eyes.

'How—quaint,' Shanna ventured before shifting her attention to Dimitri. 'I'm throwing a party tomorrow night.' She paused, then gave a sultry smile. 'My apartment. Any time after eight.'

Leanne unconsciously held her breath as she waited for him to answer.

'I don't think we can make it,' Dimitri drawled. Only Leanne, and possibly Shanna, saw that his smile didn't quite reach his eyes. 'Perhaps another time?'

Shanna recovered quickly. 'Of course, darling.'

Her make-up was perfect, Leanne noted, from the gloss covering the soft fullness of her lips, to the skilful application of eyeshadow and liner, and she was unable to suppress the uncharitable thought as to how the model shaped up first thing in the morning.

Dangerous shift—she grimaced inwardly—for it inevitably led to how often Dimitri had woken in Shanna's bed, and was closely followed by contemplation of Shanna's obvious expertise in the art of sexually pleasuring a man. It had to be light-years ahead of her own.

Leanne dearly wanted to escape, except that such an action would be observed and assessed, only to be classed as immature. So she stayed, sitting seemingly relaxed, offering a polite dissertation when the occasion demanded . . . which wasn't often, for

Shanna made it patently clear that Dimitri was the focus of her attention.

Eventually the tall model rose to her feet, gave Leanne a slight smile, pressed glossy-tipped scarlet nails to Dimitri's arm, then wafted off in a cloud of heavy perfume.

'Dance with me.'

Leanne forced herself to meet Dimitri's gaze, and her eyes were wide and unflinching as the dark, unfathomable depths conducted a steady appraisal of her features.

He took hold of her hand, threading his fingers through her own, and she felt them tighten as she attempted a surreptitious bid for freedom.

There really wasn't much she could do except comply, at least, not in public, and with a gracious smile she rose to her feet and allowed him to lead her on to the dance-floor.

She was a competent partner, possessed of a natural grace, and she moved into his arms with ease, feeling the customary surge of warmth on contact with his body.

He held her close, his hold lightly possessive, and she had the strangest feeling that if she attempted to break free he would refuse her release.

The temptation to rest her head into the curve of his shoulder was motivated by her own traitorous soul, not her mind or the pain in her heart which ensured that she danced with such utter correctness that her constricted muscles began to ache from the strain.

Dimitri didn't offer so much as a word, although once she could have sworn she felt the brush of his lips against her hair.

When the music changed, he led her back to their table, his hand firm against the small of her back.

'Would you like to leave?'

Leanne turned slightly and looked at him carefully. She didn't want to stay, but she wasn't sure she could bear to be alone with him. She knew for certain that she didn't want to share his bed ... at least, not tonight.

'Do you have an early start in the morning?' The query was polite, and she tempered it with a smile that brought a faint narrowing to his eyes.

'No earlier than usual.'

'In that case, I'll leave it up to you.'

She saw a fleeting glittering gleam in his eyes, then it was gone. 'I think we've done our duty. It will take all of thirty minutes to reach the door.'

It took slightly longer as they paused at one table, then another, exchanging words with business and social acquaintances as they went.

The Kostakidas empire commanded immense respect, as did the man who held the directorial chair. His presence at any social soirée was a considered coup, and Leanne could only admire his effortless ease in fielding several invitations to up-coming events.

She was surprised to see that it was almost midnight as Dimitri eased the Jaguar from the underground car park, and she leaned back against the head-rest.

The traffic was minimal once they left the inner-city, and she was grateful for the soft music drifting from the car's stereo system, for it precluded the necessity to make conversation.

The streets in the exclusive suburb of Toorak were quiet, and in no time at all Dimitri brought the car to a halt inside the garage.

Once indoors, he moved towards the lounge. 'A drink?'

She hesitated, then gave a slight shrug in acquiescence. Why not? It might help her sleep. 'A light brandy, with ginger ale,' she requested as she followed him into the room.

With ease he removed his tie, then slipped free the top two buttons of his shirt. The action changed his appearance quite dramatically as he shed the outer trappings of sophisticated formality.

Minutes later he placed a crystal tumbler in her hand, and she sipped from it slowly, feeling the warmth steal through her body as the alcohol began to take effect.

He projected an aura of latent power, a distinctive mesh of dangerous masculinity and sensuality that was wholly sexual.

Unbidden, a warm ache began deep inside her, slowly spreading through every vein in her body. It was damnable, incomprehensible, she mused silently, hating him more at this precise moment than she'd ever hated anyone in her life.

'Tired?'

'That's a loaded question,' Leanne responded with enforced lightness. 'How am I expected to answer?'

His eyes narrowed faintly, then assumed an expression of indolent amusement. 'Why not with honesty?'

Her lips trembled slightly, and her eyes held a tinge of aching sadness. 'I don't want to sleep with you.'

He lifted a hand to her cheek, and she flinched away from the brush of his fingers as he trailed them along the edge of her jaw, then slowly traced the throbbing cord at her neck.

The breath seemed to catch in her throat, and her eyes clung to his, bright and intensely vulnerable.

'No?'

His gentle query proved her undoing, and she moved back a pace, her body stiffening as she fought to control her emotions.

'I won't be a substitute.' Her voice was quietly angry, and she was shaking inside, caught up in a complex web that threatened to engulf her fragile senses.

'For Shanna?' Dimitri pursued silkily, and she suppressed the sudden shiver that feathered the surface of her skin.

'I don't possess her——'

'Sexual proficiency?'

Her eyes began to ache, along with the rest of her body, and she resisted the temptation to offer a flippant reply. 'I can't think of a better term,' she agreed at last.

'There's a difference between a partner who performs the sexual act like a mechanical doll, preoccupied with the monetary rewards to be gained from the relationship,' he drawled, 'And a wonderfully warm woman who loses herself in the sharing of a mutual joy.'

Her eyes widened measurably at his implication. 'That's...deplorable,' she whispered.

'The truth,' Dimitri mocked with hateful cynicism.

Without another word she finished her drink, then, after placing the tumbler carefully down on a nearby table, she turned and walked from the room, uncaring whether he followed or not.

Upstairs she entered their suite and undressed, removed her make-up, released her hair, then she pulled on a nightshirt and made her way down the hallway to the room she'd occupied as her own.

The thought of sharing the same bed, just lying there waiting for him to slide in beside her, was impossible.

She told herself she didn't care about the consequences of her action as she folded back the counterpane and slid between the sheets.

For an age she lay staring sightlessly at the ceiling, feeling hopelessly torn by a host of complex emotions.

How could you hate someone you loved? she agonised. Jealousy was hell and damnation. She had married with no illusions, so what right did she have to be *jealous*?

Leanne was on the edge of sleep when she heard the faint click of the door opening, and her heart felt as if it jumped to her throat as Dimitri crossed over to the bed.

Without a word he reached forward, removed the covers, then lifted her into his arms.

'Leave me alone!'

'If you don't want to make love, that's your prerogative,' he drawled hatefully as he walked from the room. 'But we share the same bed.'

'Doesn't it matter that I might choose not to?' she cried, sorely tried by his inherent strength and indomitable will.

'Not in the least,' he declared as he trod the short distance to their suite.

'Damn you,' she cursed, struggling to be free of him and failing miserably. 'Damn you to *hell*.'

Without a word he lowered her on to the bed, then slid in to lie beside her, and she rolled on to her side away from him, curling into a protective ball, too tense to contemplate sleep.

She remained still for what seemed an age, almost afraid to move, aware of his recumbent form mere inches away.

More than anything she would have liked to turn and flail at him with angry fists, to verbally assault him for behaving like a dominant, tyrannical *brute*. Except that if she did it would have only one ending, and her victory would be no victory at all.

CHAPTER SEVEN

LEANNE must have slept, for she woke to discover that the bed was empty. A quick glance at the bedside clock revealed that it was after eight, and with an audible groan she slid to her feet.

After a quick shower she donned cotton shorts and a top, then ran lightly down the stairs to the kitchen.

'Dimitri has already left for the city,' Eleni told her with a smile, and Leanne hid her relief as she retrieved orange juice from the refrigerator, then she crossed to the pantry for some cereal.

The day stretched ahead with very little perceived direction, and when she'd eaten she returned upstairs and changed into tailored white trousers and a matching blouse. Then she applied make-up, slid her feet into high-heeled white sandals, and caught up the keys to the Mercedes.

What she needed, she decided as she cleared the gates and began heading towards the cluster of shops and trendy boutiques at Toorak, was something constructive to do with her time.

Paige had been content to aid numerous worthwhile charities and serve on various committees. However, Leanne knew that that wasn't her scene, nor could she just stay at home doing nothing, or whiling away the hours endlessly shopping.

111

Besides which, she missed the beauty therapy clinic—the clients, the friendly staff, the contact with people.

Leanne caught sight of a parking space and slid into it. Minutes later she entered a fashion boutique and browsed idly before emerging on to the pavement.

There was a beauty clinic in the immediate vicinity, and on impulse she walked inside and requested an appointment from a receptionist who held the phone in one hand and a pencil in the other.

'Aromatherapy? I'm sorry,' the receptionist intoned with regret.

'Tomorrow?' Leanne persisted. It hardly mattered which day.

'Our aromatherapist was rushed to hospital last night for emergency surgery.' Another phone rang, and she cast it a look of flustered exasperation. 'I'm trying to locate a replacement to take our existing appointments.'

'I'm a trained aromatherapist.' The words were out before Leanne could give them much thought. 'I could fill in for you. I have my own clinic on the Gold Coast,' she added, unsure until that moment just how badly she wanted this opportunity to work out.

'You're not serious?' the other girl queried with a mixture of disbelief and hopeful reservation. 'Do you have any credentials you can show the manageress?'

'Not on me, but I can have them to you in an hour,' Leanne assured her.

'I'll call her. An hour?'

'I'll be back at ten-thirty.'

She was, with minutes to spare, and quarter of an hour later she not only had the job, but she was asked if it was possible to make an immediate start.

The day was pleasantly hectic, with a brief break at midday, during which she put a call through to Eleni to assure her that she'd be home in time for dinner.

It was almost six when she slid in behind the wheel of the Mercedes, and she eased the vehicle into the flow of traffic, feeling happier than she had in ages, for there was a sense of achievement, as well as satisfaction, in doing something she really enjoyed.

Twenty minutes later she drew to a halt behind Dimitri's Jaguar, and cut the engine. Once indoors, she let Eleni know she was back before moving quickly upstairs to shower and change.

Dimitri was in the process of discarding his jacket when she entered the bedroom, and she met his dark gaze with a cautious smile.

'Hi,' she greeted him, lifting a hand to remove the pins confining her hair, then when it fell free she raked fingers through its length and pushed a few locks back behind each ear.

'How was your day?' He loosened his tie and began unfastening the buttons on his shirt.

He knew. Eleni would have told him. Yet Leanne was unable to read anything from his expression.

'Quite different from what I expected,' she proffered with a slightly rueful smile, and proceeded to fill in the details of how she came to be employed. 'Do you mind?'

He pulled his shirt free from the waistband of his trousers, and she caught her breath in mesmerised fascination at the set of his powerful shoulders and the broad expanse of muscled chest.

'How temporary is the position?'

'I'm not sure,' Leanne offered slowly. 'A week, possibly two.' She met his gaze, and held it.

His slight smile held a degree of cynicism. 'You find the life of a wealthy socialite boring?'

'I was never a socialite,' she said evenly. 'And I didn't ask to be wealthy.'

His eyes held hers for a few seemingly long seconds, then he conducted a slow appraisal of her features before focusing on the generous curve of her mouth. 'There are occasions when it's necessary for me to entertain business associates. As my wife, you're expected to be at my side.'

'Ever the gracious hostess?'

He closed the distance between them, and, lifting a hand, he cupped her chin, tilting it slightly so that she had to look at him. 'I have no objection to your working for a few weeks, or even longer, if it's important to you. But not in the evening. Understood?'

'What about late-night shopping on Friday?'

'I won't countenance any situation where you have to walk to your car after dark,' he said hardly.

'I could——'

'It isn't negotiable, Leanne.'

'You don't have the right,' she argued, then she gasped out loud as he slid a hand beneath her hair and held fast her nape.

'Acquaint the manageress,' Dimitri insisted silkily. 'Otherwise I'll do it myself.'

Leanne twisted her head, and winced as he refused to release his hold. 'You're behaving like a dictatorial tyrant!' she accused, and her eyes flashed with the brilliance of sapphire.

'Try someone who has no desire to see you frightened or harmed in any way,' he corrected her.

'Oh...go to hell!' she flung vehemently, and there was nothing she could do to prevent the slow descent of his head, or the punishing force of his kiss.

It seared right down to her soul, becoming almost an annihilation, and she wanted to cry out against him for attempting a total conflagration of her senses.

Balling each hand into a fist, she hit him wherever she could connect—hard little punches that proved ineffectual against the taut musculature of his ribs and shoulders.

With galling ease he caught first one hand then the other and held them effortlessly behind her back, and she gave an audible groan as he caught her close in against him.

There was no escape from the relentless pressure of his mouth, or the plundering force of a kiss so intense it was almost a violation as he sought to impress his domination.

When at last he released her, Leanne stood in silence, her eyes stormy.

'Care to join me in the shower?' he taunted softly, and when she shook her head he slanted one eyebrow in silent mockery. 'Pity.'

Without a further word he slid down the zip fastening of his trousers and discarded them, tossing them over the valet-frame before moving into the *en suite*.

Leanne waited until he closed the door, then she collected fresh underwear and a change of clothes and made her way to the suite that had been her own for the past ten years.

There, she quickly showered and dressed, then, without bothering with any make-up, she moved quickly downstairs to the dining-room to help Eleni transfer serving dishes on to the table.

Dinner was a strained meal—at least as far as Leanne was concerned. She toyed with her food, forking a few morsels from the starter of vineleaf-wrapped parcels of mince and rice, ate sparingly of the excellent veal, and declined dessert.

'Not hungry?' Dimitri ventured as he selected a tempting *baklava* and transferred it on to his plate.

'Not particularly,' she answered quietly. Their conversation during the meal had been desultory at best as she tempered each response with extreme politeness.

'Don't sulk, Leanne,' he drawled, and she looked at him carefully, aware of the hard strength evident in the broad-sculptured planes of his attractively moulded features.

'I don't care to be subjugated in any way,' she ventured carefully, and he lifted one eyebrow in silent query.

'Be specific.'

The silky tone of his voice sent a sliver of ice scudding down her spine. To challenge him was the height of folly, yet she was damned if she'd meekly slip into a subservient role.

'I don't consider you have the right to lay down restrictions, or inhibit my actions,' she declared, watching as he lifted the napkin to his mouth and laid it down on the table. Each movement seemed deliberate, and his eyes never left hers for a second.

'Don't fight me,' he cautioned silkily. 'I won't allow you to win, and afterwards you may well query the wisdom of the exercise.'

'By exerting sheer male force?' she flung angrily.

His eyes resembled shards of dark obsidian ice, and she shivered at the latent anger buried beneath the surface of his control.

'*Force*, Leanne?' The single query held a degree of dangerous softness that sent a chill slithering through her veins.

Quite suddenly she had had enough, and with extreme care she got to her feet, then pushed in her chair.

'A tactical retreat?'

She looked at him carefully, almost hating him. 'If I stay here, I'll probably throw something at you.' Her mouth trembled with angry futility, and her eyes ached. Without a further word she turned and walked from the room.

It was too early to go to bed, and she had no desire to view television or read a book. Without any clear thought she moved to the rear of the house and entered the grounds.

Within minutes she was joined by Prince, the Alsatian guard-dog, and she let him nuzzle her hand before trailing her fingers up to fondle his ears. He lifted his head and playfully pawed the ground, then padded dutifully at her side as she moved through the gardens.

Trim borders, perfect blooms, and nary a weed in sight, she brooded pensively as she trod the pebbled pathway. Even the lawn was a lush green, courtesy of an automatic sprinkler system, its length clipped with meticulous precision by the dedicated George.

The pool looked cool and inviting, with covered deck-chairs placed at even intervals around its edge, and sun umbrellas still open above two tables. The light was fading as the sun sank slowly beyond the horizon, and the sky bore soft pink streaks at its edge denoting the promise of another fine day.

Without thought, she selected a lounger and sank down against its cushioned length, aware that Prince had chosen to rest on his haunches at her side.

A slight shiver shook her slim frame. There was a guard-dog at her feet, a home which resembled a fortress, and a husband who viewed her as a valued possession.

To be so involved with Dimitri Kostakidas was a terrible burden—emotionally and mentally. At this precise moment she didn't know if she wanted to be free of him or not.

Living with him was becoming a battle of wills. Yet the thought of existing without him almost sent her to the brink of despair.

Where did Shanna fit in? Was the glamorous model intent on causing trouble simply for the sake of it? Or had she genuinely believed that her relationship with Dimitri was more than just a casual affair?

Leanne sensed Prince's movement an instant before she heard his faint whine of pleasure, and she glanced up to see that Dimitri had emerged from the house and was moving towards the pool.

He walked with the easy litheness of the physically fit, and she watched as Prince rose to his feet and padded forward to greet him.

Man and beast, she mused idly as Dimitri ran a hand over the animal's body. Each as powerful as the other, and equally dangerous.

'Admiring the sunset? Or is this a means of escape?'

His voice was a quizzical drawl, and she raised solemn eyes towards his.

'Both,' she admitted succinctly.

He smiled, his lips curving at the edges as he surveyed her recumbent form. 'I came out to suggest a game of tennis.' He caught the spark of interest in her eyes before it was quickly veiled. 'We used to play together, remember?'

How could she forget? Dimitri had coached her in the evenings and at weekends in those early days, encouraging her in practice sessions so that her game lifted from the socially acceptable to an acquired edge of competitiveness. She'd partnered him against Paige and Yanis, always striving to produce her best and exalting in any praise he chose to bestow.

'Is this a desire to actually play tennis, or a veiled attempt to extend an olive-branch?' Leanne queried solemnly, watching as his eyes assumed a gleam of humour.

'What better way of throwing something at me than a racket-impelled tennis ball?'

'The best of three sets?' she countered, and saw one eyebrow slant quizzically.

'At that rate we won't finish until at least ten o'clock.'

'I plan to exhaust you.'

His laughter was deep and throaty, and she took the hand he held out, allowing him to pull her to her feet.

Leanne went indoors and changed into shorts and a top while he retrieved rackets, balls, and activated the floodlights.

She hadn't played in a while, and it seemed weeks since she'd followed her normal exercise routine.

Dimitri, on the other hand, was disgustingly fit, and it showed. The play was hardly even, yet he made no attempt to utilise his superior strength, and merely returned each ball with ease.

He won the first set by three games, and allowed the second set to reach six all before winning the tie-breaker.

'I need a cool drink, followed by a long, leisurely soak in the spa,' Leanne declared as she took the towel from him and patted moisture from her brow and neck.

It was after ten, and she was pleasantly tired. The prospect of a spa-bath was infinitely inviting, and in the kitchen she filled a glass with ice, added orange juice, then carried it upstairs.

Five minutes later she stripped off her clothes, then she switched on the jets, and stepped into the bath to enjoy the blissful sensation of tiny bubbles of pulsing warmth surging against her body.

She had little idea of the passage of time, and when the last of her drink was finished she closed her eyes in a bid for total relaxation.

'Do you intend staying there all night?' a deep voice drawled. Her lashes swept slowly open and she regarded him silently for several seconds.

He looked vaguely satanic with a dark towel hitched at his waist. Dangerous, indomitable, and displaying an indecent amount of steel-muscled flesh, she decided silently, inwardly cursing herself for taking so long.

'If you don't want to share,' Dimitri ventured with deceptive softness, 'I suggest you take the opportunity to vacate the bath . . . now.'

Her pulse-rate tripped and surged into a quickened beat at his expressed implication, and there was nothing she could do to prevent the instant flare of emotion deep within her, or the way it suffused her body.

'Could you please pass me a towel?' Was that her voice? It sounded impossibly husky, and she watched as he collected one and obligingly extended it within her reach.

'You want me to close my eyes in deference to your sense of modesty?' Dimitri taunted softly, and with concentrated effort she forced herself to meet his dark enigmatic gaze.

'Would you?'

His expression assumed a degree of musing humour. 'You have a beautiful body,' he proffered gently. 'Why should it distress you that I might like to admire it?'

A defiant sparkle lent her eyes a sapphire-like brilliance. 'How would you feel if the situation were reversed?'

'An invitation for me to drop the towel, Leanne?'

With deliberate slowness he reached for the twisted knot at his waist, and the movement galvanised her into action. In a few scant seconds she was on her feet with the towel clutched against her, uncaring that its edge dipped into the water.

'I'm not a voyeur, nor am I into the sort of titillating games in which you inevitably indulge,' she vowed, almost shaking with anger as she stepped out of the bath and wrapped the towel around her slim curves.

She made to move past him, only to come to an abrupt halt as his hands closed over her shoulders.

'Let me go,' she demanded fiercely.

He didn't, and she began to struggle as he urged her forward, his hands sliding down the smooth skin of her back, dislodging the towel seemingly without any effort at all.

'Don't——' Any further words she might have uttered in vilification were lost as his mouth closed over hers, firm and shamelessly possessive as he initiated a kiss so devastating that it was all she could do not to respond.

Then he raised his head, watching the visible play of emotions chasing across her expressive features, the soft trembling of her faintly bruised lips, and the darkness evident in her eyes.

'You'd be wise not to throw accusations you can't substantiate,' he warned silkily, and quite suddenly she had had enough.

'Your experience is vastly superior to mine,' she opined quietly, and his eyes assumed glittering amusement.

'Does it bother you?' When she didn't offer anything by way of response, he added gently, 'Or are you afraid you won't be able to catch up?'

She attempted to wrench out of his grasp, and failed miserably. 'You want to know what bothers me?' she vented with thinly veiled fury. '*You* do.' She was so angry she almost burned with it. 'Everything about you.'

His eyes swept her turbulent features, then slid down to the soft swell of her breasts before lifting to settle on her brilliant blue gaze. 'Have you ever given much thought as to *why*?'

'Damn you—*yes*,' she admitted shakily.

'But you're not willing to come to terms with your own analysis, is that it?'

'No.'

His faint smile held a strange gentleness. 'I suggest you go to bed.' He lowered his head and brushed his lips against her forehead. 'With luck, you might be asleep before I join you. Then you'll be spared my unwelcome attention.' He caught the edges of her towel and fastened them securely before placing her at arms' length.

Even now, in anger, her traitorous body craved his touch. It was as if her mind was totally divorced from the dictates of her flesh, and she shook her head in disbelief at her own contrariness as she moved past him and entered the bedroom.

Unfastening the towel, she slipped a silk night-shirt over her head, then slid in between the covers of the large bed.

How could she exult in his possession, and lose herself so totally in the sexual act? How could *he*? she agonised silently.

It was lust. A base, physical appetite devoid of any emotional involvement.

You lie, a mischievous imp inside her taunted. You love him. You always have. And your anger is a twofold entity: directed at him for successfully employing the degree of emotional coercion necessary to instigate this marriage, and at yourself, for allowing it to happen.

Leanne was almost asleep when Dimitri entered the room, and she registered the faint snap of the bedside light, followed by the slight depression of the mattress as he slid into bed.

It was crazy, but her whole body seemed to re-awaken and become achingly alive. Almost as if in silent recognition of the other half that made it whole.

She monitored her breathing, consciously forcing it into a deep, regular pattern while her heart thudded into a quickened beat.

The desire to stretch out and touch him was almost impossible to ignore, and she silently clenched her fingers in a conscious effort at control.

What would he do, she agonised, if she were to trail her fingers lightly down his ribcage, then trace the whorls of dark hair covering his chest? Travel lower, to the indentation of his navel, and explore the soft, curling hair at the apex of his thighs. Would his manhood swell beneath her touch and become rigid with need?

She closed her eyes tightly against an erotic fantasy so hauntingly vivid that her whole body took fire and began to burn.

Perhaps she could turn slightly, as if in sleep, and accidentally brush her foot against his leg. Or maybe her hand might touch his arm. She re-hearsed it in her mind, going over each individual action with the precision of a film director before discarding each and every manoeuvre as being too contrived. Besides, if he was asleep, her actions would fail to register. And she was damned if she possessed the courage actively to initiate a blatant seduction.

Slowly she willed her body to relax, persuading her mind into a state of tranquillity, and she slipped into a deep sleep where featured dreams seemed to focus on the man who occupied her conscious mind. Perhaps it was auto-suggestion, but they were lying in bed and he was gently teasing her into wakefulness. In the dream she smiled, then stretched like a playful kitten, openly inviting his touch as she murmured her approval in pleasurable anticipation of what was to follow...

Except that the veils of unconsciousness slowly began to lift, and she discovered that the dream had become reality.

For a moment she lay perfectly still, unwilling to move so much as a muscle, and the breath locked in her throat as he brushed light fingers across her breasts, circling first one, then the other, before trailing down to her waist.

When he reached her thigh she tensed, then gave a barely audible groan as his hand slipped beneath the hem of her nightshirt.

There was no thought of denial, and she turned towards him, her lips warm and generous as they met his, and their loving was long and slow and incredibly sweet.

Afterwards he gathered her close, and she rested her head against the curve of his shoulder, wanting to encapsulate this precise moment and hold it close to her heart.

CHAPTER EIGHT

LEANNE parked the Mercedes, then she walked briskly towards the beauty clinic. It was a beautiful summer's day, with a clear blue sky and the sun's warmth tempered by the slightest breeze.

There was a sense of pleasurable anticipation for the day ahead, and she greeted the receptionist with a friendly smile as she entered the clinic.

'There's an early appointment due to commence in five minutes, Leanne. The morning is well-booked, and so is the afternoon.' The receptionist checked the pencillings. 'Georgina Fyfe-Smith. Her record card is in the treatment-room.'

Leanne hurried through and donned the short-sleeved dusty-pink coat that comprised a uniform before checking the card for her client's preferred choice of aromatic oils.

Aromatherapy was becoming popular as more people benefited from its therapeutic qualities, and the selection of oils was attuned to each individual client and his or her mood.

The morning's appointments spilled into the afternoon, with one client phoning in ahead to say she'd be delayed, reducing Leanne's scheduled lunch-break to an inadequate ten minutes, just enough time for a hastily eaten sandwich and cool drink.

However, it was compensated for somewhat when her three-thirty appointment failed to arrive on time, and at three-fifty she checked with the receptionist.

'Miss Delahunty hasn't phoned in. Maybe she's been caught up in traffic.'

Shanna? It was a sufficiently unusual name to cause Leanne's stomach muscles to stiffen.

Toorak was an exclusive area, and there was a possibility that Shanna was a regular client of this particular clinic. Leanne couldn't discount the likelihood of coincidence, for word travelled fast in the social set and the clinic was a favoured haunt of several leading socialites.

At precisely four o'clock, a good thirty minutes late, the tall brunette swept into Reception in a waft of exotic perfume, her red designer outfit a stunning complement to her striking good looks.

'*Leanne*!' the model exclaimed with feigned surprise. 'You're *working* here?'

'The clinic's aromatherapist was hospitalised for surgery,' she explained quietly. 'I'm merely filling in until they find someone to take her place.'

'Noble of you, darling,' Shanna drawled.

She was a cat, Leanne decided. Pure feline, with sharpened claws poised and ready to inflict pain. Professionalism was responsible for Leanne's warm smile. 'Please come through.' Leading the way, she moved towards a private room at the rear of the main salon. 'There's a towelling robe behind the door. I'll give you a few minutes to change and make yourself comfortable.'

There was no doubt the model possessed a beautiful, lissom body, with smooth, toned muscle and excellent skin. Leanne set to work, assuring herself that the only way to get through the appointment was to disregard any personalities and simply do her job.

With luck, Shanna would lie quietly and enjoy the therapeutic qualities without feeling the need to offer anything by way of conversation.

'One wonders *why* you're working,' the brunette began, however, 'when you have a nice little fortune of your very own. Dimitri can hardly approve, surely?'

'Why should he disapprove, when it's only such a temporary arrangement?' Leanne parried carefully, loath to allow personalities to intrude.

'As is your marriage?'

Careful, an inner voice cautioned silently. 'Whatever gave you that idea?'

'Let's just say I know Dimitri well enough to be aware you couldn't satisfy him for long,' Shanna mocked.

'Really?'

'Oh, yes, darling. He likes his women receptive and provocatively inventive,' she offered sweetly.

It took all Leanne's control not to inflict a minor injury as she forced herelf to continue with the massage. 'To match his lusty appetite?'

'He's an exciting lover,' Shanna offered with a throaty laugh. 'Earthily primitive, yet displaying incredible *tendresse*. An incredibly potent combination, wouldn't you agree?'

Leanne refrained from making any comment as she selected an aromatic oil and began the gentle, rhythmic movement, focusing all her concentration on completing the therapy without allowing Shanna to rattle her composure.

'It's amazing how many of the wealthy arrange suitable marriages,' the model observed with marked cynicism. 'A husband consolidates his position and financial standing by taking a wife whose assets equal his, for wealth is power, and a required entrée into the upper social echelons. In your case, Dimitri wanted to regain control of Paige's bequest.'

It made sense. Even if it was partially untrue, it still made sense. It also sickened her to think that Shanna was only one of several people who must entertain similar views on their alliance.

However, it was impossible that Shanna knew the extent of Leanne's inheritance, just as it was equally impossible to imagine Dimitri divulging any details. Which meant the glamorous model had taken a calculated guess, and deliberately sought to inflict wilful mental damage.

At last the session was over, and Leanne left the room in order for Shanna to dress, then she forced herself to summon a friendly smile when the brunette swept out to Reception.

'I imagine I'll see you tonight,' Shanna declared, and Leanne cast her a puzzled glance. 'The opera,' Shanna informed her, slanting one eyebrow in faint disbelief. 'Dimitri has tickets. Surely he told you?'

He had, over breakfast. 'Yes, of course.' She loved the opera, and *La Bohème* was a publicised triumph featuring an excellent cast. Tonight was a much vaunted social event, where some of the cream of the city's society could be guaranteed to gather.

'No doubt I'll see you there.' Shanna's smile was wide and infinitely lethal, and it took considerable effort for Leanne to retain a semblance of calm.

Not if I see you first, she assured her silently.

'A friend of yours?' the receptionist queried as Shanna passed through the plate-glass doors.

'An acquaintance,' Leanne corrected her. 'I didn't realise she was a client of yours.'

'I know who she is, of course,' the receptionist declared. 'But I've never seen her here before.'

There was little doubt that Shanna's appearance had been a calculated attempt to unsettle Leanne's composure, and the fact hardly aided her peace of mind as she drove the short distance home.

It was hot outside, the air curiously still, and she hurried indoors with the intention of swimming a few lengths of the pool before it was time to shower and change for dinner.

'Eleni. I'm home,' she called as she headed towards the kitchen. A delicious aroma teased her nostrils, and she felt it curl down into her stomach, stimulating her appetite and causing her to bestow an appreciative commendation on the woman who was more friend than employee. 'Have I time for a swim?'

Eleni's features broke into a broad smile. 'Of course. But no more than half an hour, hmm? Dimitri rang; he will be a little late. You had a good day, yes?'

Up until an hour ago, it was fine, Leanne felt like saying, but such an answer would provoke questions, and she wasn't sure she wanted to offer any response. 'Great.' She reached for a banana, peeled it, and bit into the delicious flesh with evident enjoyment.

'Ah—you eat now?' Eleni scolded. 'I made roast lamb, with plenty vegetables, and your favourite apple crumble for dessert.'

'I'm ravenous,' Leanne assured her with a cheeky grin. 'I was so busy, I didn't get to have lunch.'

'Go have your swim,' the housekeeper bade her. 'You want I should call you?'

Leanne shook her head, then ran lightly upstairs, only to emerge five minutes later attired in a patterned silk bikini with a towel slung over one shoulder.

The water was refreshingly cool as she plunged in at the deep end, and she surfaced to stroke a leisurely pace for several lengths, exulting in the physical exertion.

She could easily have stayed there much longer, except that the need to shower and wash her hair before dinner precluded any attempt to dally, and she reluctantly swam to the pool's edge and levered herself up on to the tiled edge.

Five minutes later she was in the shower, and, after completing her ablutions, she slipped quickly into fresh underwear and blow-dried her hair before emerging into the bedroom with the intention of selecting something suitable to wear, only to come to an abrupt halt at the sight of Dimitri in the process of shedding his jacket.

'Finished in the bathroom?'

His fingers moved to loosen his tie deftly before tending to the buttons on his shirt, and she offered a monosyllabic averment as she stepped towards the capacious walk-in wardrobe, removing the first thing that came to hand from its hanger.

'Eleni said that dinner will be ready in five minutes,' he drawled, and she slid the dress over her head, then smoothed it down over her hips and fastened the zip.

'I'll go and help.' It was an escape at best, and she breathed a small sigh of relief as she descended the stairs.

Leanne was so studiously polite during dinner that it drew Dimitri's attention.

'If something is bothering you, why not tell me?'

Leanne paused from the pleasurable task of spooning a segment from Eleni's excellent apple crumble and looked at him carefully.

'Why should you think that?'

A slight smile twisted the edges of his mouth, and his eyes held discernible cynicism. 'You're determined to make this a guessing game?'

She replaced the spoon and tried to dampen the edge of her simmering anger. 'I wasn't aware we were playing a game,' she ventured, hating his ability to perceive her every mood. She arched a delicate, finely shaped eyebrow, and met his dark, enigmatic gaze with solemnity. 'Besides, you'd only be amused.'

His eyes narrowed faintly, his scrutiny dark and direct. 'Why would you imagine I'd be amused by anything that affects you?'

A faint hollow feeling settled in the region of her heart. She'd never win with Dimitri. He was too astute, too innately perceptive ever to be fooled by any smokescreen she might attempt to create.

'It's nothing I can't handle,' Leanne revealed with a imperceptible shrug.

'I have little doubt you can,' he drawled musingly.

'Such faith you have,' she mocked, and a gleam of humour lit his dark eyes, deepening the lines radiating from each corner, and teasing the edges of his mouth.

'You're a beautiful young woman,' he told her softly. 'Possessed of a generous soul. If anyone were to deliberately hurt you, they'd have to answer to me.'

Somehow she had to inject some levity into the situation, for if she didn't she'd go to pieces, and that would never do. 'Does that mean I should make a list?'

'I'm perfectly serious.'

She pondered on his reaction if she were to reveal that his ex-lover was the source, then decided against it. 'If you've finished, I'll clear everything on to the trolley and take it through to the kitchen,' she indicated, and, standing, she began stacking plates and gathering cutlery.

'Leave it. There isn't time,' Dimitri instructed, and she gave a helpless shrug as Eleni came bustling into the room.

Upstairs Leanne tended to her make-up, swept her hair into an elegant knot atop her head, then changed into a classically designed red evening suit that highlighted the texture of her skin and the slenderness of her delicate curves. Slipping her feet into matching shoes, she gathered up an evening bag and turned towards Dimitri.

The sight of him attired in a formal black evening suit, white silk shirt and black bow-tie made her catch her breath.

He was a ruggedly handsome man whose broad, sculpted features were a visual attestation to an enviable mix of inherited genes. Yet there was so much more apparent than mere physical good looks, for he emanated an aura of power and inherent strength together with a heightened degree of latent sexuality. A quality that was instantly recognisable to women, most of whom deliberately sought to arouse his attention... if only to assert their own femininity.

Dangerous, she decided, unable to still the thrill of pleasure that stole through her body as she preceded him from the house and took her seat in the car.

Yanis had possessed remarkably similar qualities, Leanne mused as Dimitri fired the powerful engine and sent the vehicle purring down the driveway. Yet her stepfather had had eyes only for Paige.

To want that kind of love for herself was akin to wishing for the moon.

Damn, she cursed shakily. Such introspection was not only detrimental, it was downright disruptive. Far better to concentrate on the passing scenery, and ponder on the pleasure of experiencing a performance of *La Bohème*.

The State Theatre comprised three levels in a hall reminiscent in design and décor of the elegant European eighteenth-century opera houses, and Leanne sat enthralled through the love duet between Rodolfo and Mimi at the end of Act One.

'Enjoying the performance?' Dimitri queried as the lights came on, and she directed a stunning smile at him.

'The cast is superb, and the music...' Her eyes were a dazzling blue, radiating intense pleasure. 'I love it,' she concluded without reserve, and her eyes widened in surprise as he took hold of her hand and lifted it to his lips to caress each finger in turn.

There was something infinitely sensual in the gesture, and her mouth trembled slightly as she met his dark, gleaming gaze and caught a glimpse of latent passion in their depths.

'Would you like a drink?'

There hadn't been time for coffee after dinner, and she was thirsty. 'Please.'

It seemed that several patrons entertained the same idea, and the foyer was impossibly crowded, so that managing a clear passage to the bar became a test of endurance.

'Dimitri! How *wonderful* to see you,' a voice shrieked—feminine, of course, Leanne registered as the owner carved a path towards them.

Krissie Van Hahme, hostess extraordinaire, and unequalled in the society stakes. She was also a tireless worker for charity, and a friend of Paige.

'Leanne, darling,' she greeted her, leaning forward to bestow a kiss on each cheek as Dimitri excused himself in a quest to fetch liquid refreshments. 'So sad about your dearest mother. She was an asset, such a marvellous asset. An inspiration to us all.' She caught hold of Leanne's hand. 'I heard the news of your marriage, and I'm delighted. Truly delighted.'

Effusive, gregarious, but utterly sincere, the widow had more money than she knew what to do with, and regarded its excess as slightly obscene, choosing to compensate for her late husband's avaricious acquisition of it by donating large amounts to worthwhile charities, and compounding such compensation by tirelessly serving on several committees.

'Thanks, Krissie,' Leanne returned. 'How are you?'

'Busy, darling. But that's the way I prefer to be. And you're looking so well—stunning,' she qualified. 'Love is a wonderful aphrodisiac, and I just know it won't be long before you'll fill that beautiful home with children. Paige would have adored grandchildren.' She brightened, and cast Leanne a beautiful smile. 'There are a few functions prior to Christmas. I'll send Dimitri the usual invitations. Now, if you'll excuse me?'

Leanne managed a suitable response as her mind reeled with the implications of Krissie's words.

Children. She hadn't thought that far ahead. *Why* hadn't she? she agonised, shocked into the realisation that if she bore Dimitri a child he'd never let her go, much less the child. Then she'd be trapped in a loveless marriage where her inimical husband held all the cards. Was she only a pawn in a manipulative game controlled by a man who wanted to continue a dynasty? Had that been part of his motive in contriving first the engagement, then the marriage?

'Your drink.'

Leanne heard Dimitri's familiar drawl, and turned slightly to take the cool glass from his hand. 'Thanks.'

'We have only a few minutes before commencement of the second act,' he indicated, turning slightly as someone greeted him by name.

Leanne was glad of the distraction, for it enabled her to sip the mineral water without his scrutiny, and it was a relief when the electronic warning sounded, alerting patrons that the intermission was about to conclude.

Instead of giving the main players her undivided attention, she focused on the stormy love-affair between the secondary characters, identifying with the portrayal of passion and anger, for in some measure it resembled the tumult within her own heart.

The foyer appeared less crowded during the intermission between Acts Two and Three, and it was a pleasure to catch sight of one of her friend's parents and hear news of their daughter's sojourn in Europe.

Not so pleasant was Shanna's appearance at Dimitri's side, and Leanne felt she should be commended for her acting ability as she offered the model a polite greeting.

There were several words equally suitable with which to describe the beautiful brunette, but Leanne could only think of one. Gorgeous. From the top of her head to the tips of her toes, she was a visual attestation to stunning beauty. Everything was superbly co-ordinated; her designer-label gown and handmade matching shoes; jewellery; make-up.

Poised at Dimitri's side, Shanna looked his perfect complement, for her height in slender high heels brought the top of her head level with his eyes.

She doesn't possess an insecure bone in her body, Leanne thought silently. She has fame, fortune, and every endowment nature could bestow.

Yet she didn't have Dimitri. Or did she? Was she content to wait on the sidelines, willing to accept whatever attention he could offer whenever circumstances permitted, until a decent length of time elapsed and Dimitri sought a divorce? Maybe Shanna didn't consider marriage that important . . .

No, Leanne decided bleakly. Shanna would want it all. She was merely a temporary hindrance in the glamorous model's scheme of things.

'No, I don't think so,' Leanne heard Dimitri's deep, drawling tones as she brought her attention back to the present. 'We both have an early start tomorrow.'

His hand rested lightly at the base of Leanne's spine, and she felt its soothing movement as he trailed his fingers to her waist.

Shanna's eyes narrowed slightly, and she made a faint *moue*. 'That rarely stopped you visiting a nightclub after a show in the past.'

'I prefer to spend the time making love to my wife.'

There was no visible sign of Shanna's anger as she allowed a soft, tinkling laugh to emerge from her lips. 'All cats are alike in the dark.'

'You think so?' Dimitri parried lightly. 'Would you care to parallel that axiom to each of your lovers?'

Shanna lifted a hand and laid a perfectly lacquered red nail on the lapel of Dimitri's jacket. 'You want me to declare you the best, darling?' she asked softly. 'In the presence of your wife?'

Without missing a beat, Dimitri removed Shanna's hand and released it, his expression a polite façade that fooled no one, least of all Leanne, who felt positively sickened by the exchange.

'A graceful retreat is called for, don't you think?' he ventured with dangerous silkiness, the *double entendre* unmistakable, and, with a brilliant smile, the model murmured her excuses and melted through the milling crowd.

Leanne gave a slight start as the signal alerting the end of the intermission sounded, and she forced herself to walk at Dimitri's side as he led her back into the theatre.

Within minutes of being seated the curtain rose, and Leanne stared sightlessly at the stage, the movement, the music washing over her in seemingly discordant array, for, despite the visual parade before her eyes, all she could see was the scene between Shanna and Dimitri.

She sat perfectly still, wishing with all her heart that she could get to her feet and make a dignified exit. Damn him, damn them both, she raged inwardly.

Such was the extent of her anger that she curled the fingers of one hand into the palm of her hand, then winced as the tips of her nails bit into the soft flesh.

Without warning Dimitri reached out and covered her hand with his own, and she immediately attempted to wrench it free. But his grasp assumed the strength of tensile steel, forbidding escape, and short of making a scene she had no choice but to sit in strained silence.

Her heart thudded loudly in her chest, deepening with every beat until she felt as if her entire body was a pulsing drum, and she gave a visible start as his fingers began tracing a soothing pattern over the throbbing veins at her wrist.

Leanne turned towards him, her eyes brilliant with unshed tears, then she focused her attention on the players immediately ahead.

It was a relief when Act Three concluded, and she rose to her feet at once, only to have him unbend his lengthy frame, giving every indication of accompanying her into the lobby.

As soon as they gained the aisle she attempted to tug her hand free, barely resisting the temptation to stamp on his toes in sheer frustration when he refused to permit her freedom.

'Do you mind?' she vented quietly between clenched teeth. 'Where I'm going, no man is allowed.'

He shot her a dark, assessing glance, then released her, and she moved quickly towards the powder-room. Afterwards she crossed to the mirror and freshened her lipstick, then, taking a deep, calming breath, she emerged into the lobby.

It was late by the time they reached the car, and Leanne sat in silence as Dimitri eased the vehicle from the car park and entered the flow of traffic vacating the city.

They hardly spoke during the short drive home, and once indoors she moved towards the stairs, only to come to an abrupt halt as hard fingers caught hold of her arm and swung her round to face him.

She didn't say a word, just threw him an icy look before drawing deliberate attention to the grasp he maintained on her arm.

His eyes bored into hers, his expression ruthlessly hard. 'My relationship with Shanna was over long ago.'

She felt cold, almost chilled, despite the warmth of the summer evening. 'It's of no interest to me whatsoever,' she managed coolly, holding his gaze, her eyes silently at war with his own.

'Isn't it?' Dimitri pursued with deadly softness.

Her nerves were a quivering mess in the face of his pitiless implacability, and she was conscious of the quickened pulse at the base of her throat. A visible giveaway that defied any attempt at control.

'You want to conduct a post-mortem of your exchange with Shanna?' she demanded, aware of the watchfulness apparent beneath his inscrutable façade. 'For what purpose, Dimitri? It won't change a thing.'

'It wasn't my intention for you to be hurt.'

'In order to be hurt, you have to care,' she offered seriously, attempting to lighten the words with a slight smile and failing miserably.

'And you don't?'

His faint cynicism stung, and a tinge of pink stained her cheeks as she experienced a renewed sense of helpless anger.

'Whatever you did and with whom prior to our marriage is none of my business.'

'Expertly fielded,' Dimitri mocked as he watched the agitated pulse-beat at the base of her throat.

She was unaware of the depth of her eyes and their dilation, and the soft trembling of her mouth. She only knew the futility of pain, and the power of this one man to wield it.

If she didn't escape now, she'd resort to unenviable rage or break into ignominious tears, and there was no dignity in puffy red eyes and uncontrollable emotion. Rage would inevitably bring retribution, and she knew she'd never be able to deal with its aftermath.

'It's late, and I'd like to go to bed,' she managed evenly, and there was a mesmeric silence, intensifying until she became conscious of every breath she took.

His eyes darkened measurably for a few long seconds, then his fingers loosened their hold, and she turned away from him, ascending the stairs with deliberate economy of movement.

Inside their suite she quickly discarded her clothes, unpinned her hair, then cleansed her face of make-up before pulling on a nightshirt and slipping between the sheets.

Dimitri entered the room as she was on the edge of sleep, and she heard the rustle of fabric, followed minutes later by the soft depression of the mattress as he slid in beside her.

If he reached for her, she'd turn on him like an angry cat, and her whole body tensed as she waited for him to make a move. When he didn't she became mildly resentful, conversely willing him to begin something that would give her the opportunity to exhaust some of her hidden anger.

Soon she heard the soft, steady sound of his breathing, and it rankled unbearably to think that he'd calmly summoned sleep without any effort at all.

Consequently it was ages before she relaxed sufficiently to follow his example, and when she woke it was after seven and she was alone.

CHAPTER NINE

LEANNE wasn't sure precisely what prompted her to be contrary. Maybe it wasn't any *one* thing, but a combination of several.

It began over breakfast when Eleni passed on a message from Dimitri to the effect that he expected her to join him in entertaining an associate over dinner that evening.

'I don't think I can make it,' Leanne prevaricated, damned if she would fall in graciously with his every whim.

'No?' Eleni queried, managing to inject surprise and disbelief into one word. 'You are working late?'

'I've already made tentative arrangements to meet a friend for dinner.' Until this minute, such a thought hadn't entered her head.

'Maybe you can change it for another night,' Eleni suggested, and Leanne pretended to consider, then she shook her head slightly in an expressive gesture of doubt.

'Perhaps.' She summoned a sweet smile that was meant to convey innocence. 'Would you mind phoning Dimitri? I have a busy day ahead of me, and I probably won't be able to make the call.'

She was a fool, she chastised herself an hour later as she showed the first client of the day into the treatment-room.

By mid-morning she was convinced of it, and expected every ring of the phone at Reception to herald a call from Dimitri demanding that she cancel any prior arrangement.

At noon, when the receptionist alerted her to a private call, it was almost an anticlimax.

'Take the name and number,' Leanne said quietly. 'I'll call back when I've finished with my client.'

By the time she put the call through she was a nervous wreck, and her fingers tightened round the receiver as Dimitri picked up the extension.

'Eleni says you've made plans to dine out tonight,' he said without preamble, and Leanne immediately summoned his forceful features to mind. His leashed strength seemed to emanate from him down the line, and she was unable to suppress a shiver of apprehension.

'Yes,' she responded with extreme politeness.

'With a friend, I understand.'

'I do have friends, Dimitri,' she said drily. 'Is it so surprising that I might like to share a meal and a few hours with one of them?'

'Not at all,' he drawled. 'Invite her to join us for dinner another evening.'

She couldn't resist the faint taunt. 'Why so sure my friend is female?'

'Bravado, Leanne?' he queried with dangerous softness, and she gripped the receiver more tightly in an effort to dampen her anger. 'I'm sure your friend will understand when you explain.'

'Are you implying that *my* plans are unimportant?' She was mad, stark, raving mad to parry words with him, but she couldn't restrain herself.

'Don't play games,' he chided silkily, and she retaliated swiftly,

'Why don't you entertain him alone, Dimitri? I fail to see why you need me...unless it's a deliberate ploy to disarm him with my charm. Is the deal dependent on providing female distraction?' She paused imperceptibly, then honed in for the kill. 'Is that the role Shanna used to play?'

She sensed rather than heard his husky imprecation, and his voice was velvet-encased steel.

'I would appreciate it if you'd postpone your arrangements.'

It was as well they weren't in the same room, otherwise she knew he would exact retribution of a kind that would emphasise her foolishness in choosing to oppose him. The distance lent her the courage to proffer, 'I'll think about it.'

'Perhaps you could be sufficiently considerate to let me know your decision?'

He was angry. Furious, she amended. And she was in the grip of some crazy form of temporary insanity.

'I have a client waiting,' she informed him, and it was true. She had bookings back to back throughout the entire day. 'And it's difficult to make personal calls.' Very gently she replaced the receiver, experiencing a mixture of apprehension and exhilaration that lasted all afternoon.

At five she rang Eleni and left a message that she would be home in an hour, and it was just after six when the Mercedes drew to a halt in the garage.

The exhilaration had completely dissipated, and in its place was a knot of fearful apprehension as she entered the house and made her way upstairs.

Dear God, what had she been thinking of? To have challenged him was some form of divine madness, she railed at herself silently.

The bedroom was empty, and she released the breath she'd unconsciously been holding, only to catch it again as she heard the shower running in the adjoining bathroom.

There was no time for hesitation, and she crossed the room to the walk-in wardrobe. With shaking fingers she removed her clothes and pulled on a silk robe, then she gathered fresh underwear, tights, and flung them on to the bed.

She was about to return to the wardrobe to select something suitable to wear when Dimitri emerged from the bathroom with a towel hitched carelessly at his waist.

Her eyes flew straight to his, and her stomach completed a series of somersaults at the hard implacability evident in those dark depths.

'I leave in thirty minutes. With or without you.' His voice held a hateful drawling quality as he crossed the room and extracted underwear and socks from appropriate drawers.

Leanne hastily averted her gaze as he loosened the towel and let it drop to the floor, and she carried the mental image of his powerfully muscled frame as she fled into the bathroom.

She was ready in time, but only just, dressed in a peacock-green silk brocade gown, matching shoes, a small emerald pendant at her neck. Her hair was left loose, simply because it was easier to brush it than fasten it in a knot atop her head. As it was she was fixing her earrings in place as she descended the stairs at his side.

In the car she sat in silence, hating the icy chasm that seemed to widen between them with every passing kilometre.

'Shall we effect a truce?' Dimitri queried with deadly softness endless minutes later, and she turned towards him, seeing the hard planes of his rough-hewn profile, the splendid assemblage of tautened muscle and bone.

'You shouldn't have played the heavy husband,' she asserted quietly.

He spared her a swift, analytical glance as the traffic slowed, then directed his attention back to the road.

Minutes later he drove into the entrance of a city hotel, arranged valet parking, then crossed to her side as they entered the restaurant.

'Your guest is already here,' the *maître d'* informed them as he led the way to their table.

A tall, extremely attractive man rose to his feet and Dimitri made the introductions before seeing Leanne into her seat.

Leon Andre murmured something in French, then laughed softly as he caught her faint blush.

'I see you understand.' He smiled without a hint of remorse for the daring compliment, and his eyes held twinkling humour as they roved with expressive pleasure over her petite frame. 'If you were my wife, I wouldn't leave you languishing at home alone.'

He was nice, and almost Dimitri's equal. It was clear they were friends of long standing, and one could understand why. Both men possessed the same degree of inherent power, as well as laying claim to more than their fair share of dynamic masculinity.

'You aren't married?' Leanne queried politely, and caught his wry smile.

'I was, once. Several years ago, when I was young enough to believe I could conquer everything in sight. Unfortunately, in order to do so, I badly neglected the one person who was more important to me than all the successful deals in the world. I was too blind to see what was happening, and she left me.'

'I'm sorry,' she said with sincerity.

'I believe you are,' Leon drawled, shifting his gaze to Dimitri. 'Be careful, my friend,' he warned him with deliberate ambiguity.

'I value what I have,' Dimitri declared with silky emphasis, and the other man gave a husky laugh.

'Yes, I think you do.' He cast Leanne a musing smile. 'I'll defer to your choice of wine.'

'Oh, no,' she declined with a faint smile. 'I won't allow you to hang that one on me. You might not approve.'

'Surprise me.'

She spared Dimitri a glance and was unable to determine anything from his bland expression. 'A Pinot chardonnay?' she offered, and her eyes widened fractionally as Leon ordered an expensive import.

'So, tell me,' he began with indolent charm. 'How long have you known this adversary of mine?'

'Ten years,' she revealed with hesitation.

'Ah.' Leon sighed. 'You were too young to be swept off your feet, so he went away and allowed you to grow up.'

Leanne's mobile mouth moved to form an infectious smile. 'Right characters, wrong script. I went away and grew up.'

'He didn't pursue you?'

The wine waiter appeared, proffered the bottle, and at an indicative nod from Leon he tended to the uncorking, soliciting Leon's approval before completing his task.

'Not until recently.' Leanne lifted her glass and took an appreciative sip.

'Shall we order?' Dimitri queried with imperturbable calm.

The food was delectable, each course a superb masterpiece in taste and decorative flair. Leanne couldn't remember enjoying herself as much in ages. Perhaps it was the wine, or the light, bantering exchange Leon deliberately sought to maintain, but she found herself caught up in a mild flirtation which saw her eyes sparkle with delicious humour and her mouth curve with laughter.

'I thought this was meant to be a business dinner,' she said when the waiter served coffee.

'The business was conducted this afternoon,' Leon enlightened her with a lazy smile. 'Tonight is wholly social. Dimitri and I have known each other since our days in university. I wanted to meet the woman who'd managed to bring him to his knees.' His features softened measurably and there was no cynicism apparent in his smile. 'His choice is estimable. You're enchanting.'

She smiled faintly, and Leon chuckled, a deep, husky sound that was synonymous with the man himself.

Draining the last of his coffee, Leon spared his watch a glance, then signalled for the bill. 'Shall we take in the nightclub on the top floor?'

'Leanne?' Dimitri's voice was a soft drawl, and she found it impossible to determine anything from his expression.

It was only ten, and she didn't feel in the least tired. 'Perhaps for an hour?'

'Why not midnight?' Leon parried. 'Then you can escape before Dimitri's Jaguar turns into a pumpkin.'

The nightclub was well-patronised, the band excellent, and it seemed an age since she'd felt so alive.

'Would you like to dance?'

They had been seated for more than ten minutes, and the beat of the music was intoxicating. 'With you?'

Leon laughed softly. 'Of course with me.'

'Dimitri?' She had to ask, and his drawled consent held a tinge of humour.

Leon was amazingly light on his feet for such a tall man, and his movements were uncontrived.

'I'm not terribly good at this,' Leanne apologised, and he grinned down at her.

'You don't normally frequent nightclubs?'

'Hardly ever,' she owned. 'My preference lies with the cinema, the theatre and the ballet.'

'And in between you stay home and watch television or read a good book?'

She laughed. 'How did you guess?'

'Dimitri is a lucky man,' he remarked softly.

There wasn't a thing she could say, and in desperation she murmured, 'Perhaps we should go back.'

The band took a small break, and when they resumed Dimitri caught hold of her hand and led her on to the floor.

Dancing with Leon had been fun, but with Dimitri she was aware of the seductive pull of sexual chemistry, and she made no demure when he pulled her close. It was all too easy to lift her arms and melt in against him as they drifted to the music.

This was where she wanted to be, and she felt strangely bereft when he disentangled her arms and led her back to the table.

Leon was engrossed in conversation with an attractive redhead, and he made an introduction, then showed no surprise when Dimitri declared an intention to leave.

'*Au revoir*, Leanne,' Leon bade her gently. 'I'll see you next time I'm in town.'

'You must come to dinner.' The invitation slid easily from her lips, and he smiled.

'Thank you.' He turned towards Dimitri. 'Take good care of her.'

'Don't doubt that I shall.'

Once in the car she sat in silence, and leaned back against the head-rest as the powerful vehicle purred towards Toorak.

'A nightcap?' Dimitri queried when they were indoors, and Leanne shook her head.

She wanted to say how much she'd enjoyed the evening, but she couldn't quite bring herself to evince pleasure in another man's company. Besides, there was a dark watchfulness apparent in Dimitri's eyes that she was unable to fathom.

'I trust your friend wasn't too disappointed when you had to change your arrangements?'

His voice was a silky drawl that seemed to reach right down into the pit of her stomach, and she lifted her head slightly and met his gaze with fearless resolve.

'I hadn't made any prior arrangements for tonight,' she informed him with studied calm. 'I resented your high-handedness, and wasn't prepared to act the part of a submissive appendage who fell in with your every command.'

His eyes hardened fractionally, and his mouth curved to form a mocking smile. 'An act of defiance?'

She looked at him carefully, and refused to be intimidated by his inherent strength of will. 'Yes.'

He moved forward until he was within touching distance, and she restrained the urge to turn and run upstairs.

'It didn't bother you that such behaviour might incur my anger?' he queried with dangerous softness, and her chin lifted fractionally.

'Not at the time, no.'

Dimitri's lips curved slightly as he lifted a hand to her hair and tucked a few tendrils back behind her ear. 'And now?'

She gave a small, helpless shrug, and was unable to prevent the traitorous pull of her body towards his. It was almost as if some celestial power had predestined them as two halves of a whole, and an exigent magnetism was intent on drawing them together. 'What good will it do to fight you?'

He took in the faint wariness in the set of her mouth, the determination apparent in those beautiful blue eyes, and stated gently, 'Yet you'd like to.'

'You do tend to have that effect on me.'

He smiled, and she almost died at the degree of lazy humour evident in that dark gaze. 'Have you ever attempted to analyse *why*?'

Innate honesty provided the courage for her to offer a trifle sadly, 'I did that four years ago.' She forced herself to hold his gaze, although she was unable to prevent her lips from trembling slightly, and her eyes widened as he lifted a hand and traced the lower edge with his thumb.

She stood motionless as he lowered his head, and she closed her eyes as his mouth touched hers.

His lips were firm and warm, caressing with a sensual expertise that made the blood sing in her veins, and she became lost, an easy prey to her own treacherous emotions as he deepened the kiss, drawing her in close against him so that she couldn't help but be aware of his arousal.

Minutes later he dragged his mouth away, then with one easy movement he swept an arm beneath her knees and carried her upstairs.

I don't care, Leanne assured herself hazily. Right now, all I want is his possession, and the sharing of something so special, so magical, it transcends rational thought.

In the bedroom their clothes were an impossible encumbrance they hastily shed, and there was a hunger in his passion, an urgency that forbade a long, leisurely entrapment of the senses. There was only immediate need, and she exulted in his erotic plunder, clinging to him in rapt abandon as he took her to the edge and beyond, then held her there for the orgasmic explosion and its shuddering aftermath.

A long time later she felt the brush of his lips against the curve of her shoulder as he trailed a path to her breast to conduct a slow, sensual tasting that brought a renewed surge of emotion, and she wound her arms round his neck, holding him close as he embarked on a gentle loving that left her feeling warm and infinitely cherished.

Not cherished, an inner voice protested as she slipped slowly towards sleep. Cherish meant love, and he felt little more for her than a healthy degree of lust.

CHAPTER TEN

LEANNE entered the beauty clinic early on Saturday morning with a vague feeling of regret. Today was the last day of her temporary employment, for the manageress had been successful in engaging a satisfactory replacement who was due to start on Monday.

In a way she felt vaguely regretful, for she'd genuinely enjoyed working in the clinic, the contact with clients and the pleasure derived from their voiced appreciation. It made her aware of how much she missed her own clinic on the Gold Coast. Although Melbourne would always be home.

'You're fully booked,' the receptionist informed her with a rueful smile as Leanne paused to check the day's appointments.

The pencillings were distinct, and Leanne's heart sank as she saw that Shanna had arranged another aromatherapy session in the latter half of the morning.

It was unlikely that the glamorous model valued Leanne's services to the extent of making another appointment within the space of a few days. Which meant that Shanna had to have an ulterior motive. And there could be no doubt that the motive was centred on Dimitri.

Another gibe? Leanne pondered wryly as she checked the time a few hours later. Shanna was already ten minutes late. Was it a deliberate ploy to unsettle her?

Dammit, she scolded herself silently. She was becoming positively paranoid where Shanna was concerned.

'Leanne. Miss Delahunty is here.'

She thanked the receptionist and stepped briskly through to the foyer.

'Shanna. How are you?' she greeted her politely.

The model's smile was a practised facsimile as she swept through to the treatment-room.

With dedicated care Leanne set to work, grateful that Shanna seemed disinclined to offer much in the way of conversation.

But her gratitude was short-lived because on conclusion of the session, Shanna placed a detaining hand on her arm.

'I wonder if you might do me a favour?'

Sheer good manners forced Leanne to proffer a polite response. 'If I can,' she said cautiously, and glimpsed the gleam of satisfaction in the model's dark eyes.

'It's a rather delicate matter,' Shanna intimated, effecting a slight *moue*. One eyebrow arched, and her expression became faintly pitying. 'I considered despatching a special messenger,' she declared, 'then decided against it, unsure that Dimitri's secretary wouldn't open the package.'

Get to the point, Leanne wanted to scream, feeling very much like a cornered mouse confronted by a predatory cat who was bent on prolonging the agony of an imminent attack.

'After much deliberation, I feel it's best if I hand it to you.'

The brunette made no move to extract anything from her bag, and Leanne stood perfectly still, her eyes level, a polite smile firmly pinned in place. The effort almost killed her, but she was damned if she'd let Shanna gain so much as a glimpse of her distress.

'I was with Dimitri yesterday,' Shanna continued, moving in for the figurative kill. 'And...' she paused for deliberate effect '...one thing led to another. You know how it is?' she said archly with a negligent shrug.

Ice seemed to invade Leanne's veins, and she shivered, aware from the satisfied gleam in Shanna's eyes that she'd glimpsed the faint *frisson* of discomfort.

With almost theatrical precision the model reached into her bag and extracted two keys. 'Dimitri will want these back.'

Leanne took them from Shanna's extended hand and thrust them quickly into her pocket. She even managed a smile as she concluded the appointment.

'Management have found a replacement aromatherapist,' she informed her politely. 'Suzanne will start Monday.' Without waiting for Shanna's comment, she turned and left the treatment-room.

A short while later Shanna swept out, and Leanne checked the appointment book before taking an early lunch-break, during which she merely picked at the delectable chicken salad sandwich, and opted for a second cappuccino, holding the cup in both hands as if finding solace in the transmitted heat from the milky coffee.

The magazine she'd bought didn't hold her interest, and she merely flicked through the pages, seeing only Dimitri's classic features and those of

Shanna, intermingled in numerous poses, all of which aroused damnable jealousy.

Somehow she managed to get through the afternoon, and she was quite touched when the manageress presented her with a gift at the end of the day.

The thought of dining out tonight was the last thing she needed, she decided as she fired the engine and eased the Mercedes on to the road.

The evening's function was to be held in the glittering ballroom of a modern city hotel. Everyone who was *anyone* would attend, dressed in their finest, and it would be strictly smile-time as she mixed and mingled at Dimitri's side.

How would he react if she said she was tired and had a headache? she brooded as she drove the short distance home.

Leanne turned into their street seconds ahead of Dimitri's Jaguar, and after passing through the electronic gates she had the craziest urge to accelerate up the driveway and come to a screeching halt. Childish, she dismissed. Utterly childish.

So she eased the Mercedes forward with her customary care, and drove into the garage.

Dimitri was waiting for her as she gained the front entrance, and she registered the short-sleeved white knit shirt and tennis shorts. He possessed a superb physique, all honed muscle and deeply tanned flesh. An arresting force, she admitted silently. It was little wonder Shanna was loath to let him go.

'How was your day?'

His low-pitched drawl was accompanied by a smile, and she returned it, summoning all her acting ability to the fore as she responded, 'Interesting. And yours?'

His eyes narrowed fractionally as he detected the slight edge of cynicism, and he subjected her to an assessing appraisal. 'Physical,' he enlightened her drily. 'A few rounds of golf prior to lunch, followed by three sets of tennis this afternoon.'

They entered the main foyer together, and Leanne moved towards the staircase.

'What time do you want to leave?' Her hand went automatically to the banister as she mounted the first step, only to come to an abrupt halt as Dimitri's fingers closed over her wrist.

'What happened today?' he demanded in a voice that was deceptively soft, and she turned to look at him—a mistake, for he looked far too close for comfort.

'Why should you imagine anything happened?' she parried lightly, and suffered his scrutiny.

'You forget,' he drawled softly. 'I can read you like an open book.'

'How devastating,' Leanne responded with dry mockery. 'I have no secrets at all.'

'Meaning that I have?'

She held his gaze unflinchingly for several long seconds, then she lifted both shoulders in an ineffectual shrug. 'You give nothing away, Dimitri, other than what you choose.'

His eyes narrowed fractionally. 'Elucidate, Leanne.'

'Let me go,' she commanded quietly, hating him for being so acutely astute. She'd never been very good at masking her feelings, and she coveted his ability to present an impenetrable façade. Anger bubbled at the surface, and she closed her eyes against the force of it, only to open them again as she attempted to tug her hand free.

'When you tell me what's bothering you.'

Her eyes flashed blue fire, and there were twin flags of colour staining her cheeks as she regarded him with angry defiance.

'You're not my keeper.'

'Indisputably your husband,' Dimitri drawled, and she reined in her temper with difficulty.

'Perhaps you'd be advised to keep that in mind,' she said stiffly, and saw his eyes harden.

'I'm inclined to demand an explanation.'

Tangling with him was akin to banging her head against a brick wall; not only fruitless, but painful. 'Word gets around,' she began after a measurable silence. 'Shanna made an appointment for aromatherapy early this week, and repeated it again this morning.'

His gaze didn't falter. 'Is that an unusual occurrence?'

Leanne closed her eyes, then slowly opened them again. 'The receptionist revealed that she isn't a regular client.'

He stood waiting, his eyes dark and unfathomable. 'Don't stop there, Leanne.'

'Shanna requested that I return something to you.' It was amazing that her voice sounded so calm, when inside she was consumed with anger.

'Then whatever it is I suggest you give it to me,' he said silkily.

Without another word she reached into her shoulder-bag and withdrew the set of keys, then solemnly handed them to him.

'She said she forgot to give them to you yesterday,' she ventured drily.

'Naturally, Shanna didn't enlighten you as to their purpose.'

It wasn't a question, merely a statement, and her stomach curled at the pitiless quality in his voice.

'Tell me,' Dimitri bade her with dangerous quietness. 'What do you imagine these keys unlock?'

She didn't answer, and his eyes assumed a ruthless intensity that was almost frightening.

'My apartment?' he asked.

There was a painful lump in her throat that precluded speech, and her lips parted, only to close again as she effected a helpless shrug. Then she gasped out loud as his fingers tightened painfully on her wrist.

'What the hell are you doing?' Leanne cried as he exerted sufficient pressure to force her out to the car.

'Get in,' he directed brusquely. 'Or I'll physically place you in the seat and fasten the belt.'

'Dimitri——'

Hard hands shifted to her shoulder as he opened the passenger door.

'All right,' she capitulated with exasperation, and her fingers shook as she tended to the seatbelt while he closed the door.

Seconds later he slid in behind the wheel and fired the engine, sending the car towards the gates with a muted roar.

It took five minutes to reach his apartment block, and a further five to park the car and ride the lift to his penthouse suite on the uppermost floor.

'Here are the keys,' Dimitri said with deceptive quietness, extending them in one hand. 'Open the door.'

Leanne looked at him, saw his deadly strength of purpose, and took the keys.

The first one didn't fit. Nor did the second. Instead the security alarm went off, loud and clearly distinguishable. And it didn't stop until he inserted a coded plastic disk and punched in a series of numbers.

Her heart set up a crazy beat as it hammered against her ribs, and she almost cried out as he impelled her inside.

The door closed with a refined clunk, and she watched as he crossed to an in-house phone, lifted the handset and punched in a few digits. Quietly, distinctly, he identified himself and assured the security man that there hadn't been an attempted break-in.

Then he turned and surveyed her with cold amusement. 'Look through the apartment, Leanne.'

'No,' she refused, hating him, hating herself. But most of all hating Shanna for initiating just this scene.

'Then I'll do it with you.'

Suiting words to action, he led her into first one bedroom, then the other, pulling open drawers, flinging wide one capacious wardrobe after another, insisting on her inspection.

There was nothing remotely resembling feminine apparel anywhere. Only a variety of masculine clothing that was obviously his.

Her eyes began to ache, and she blinked to ease the emotional strain.

'Whenever I've chosen to take a woman to bed, it hasn't been here,' Dimitri informed her with uncompromising inflexibility. 'Shanna handed you keys to a leased apartment and underground car park.' He paused imperceptibly. 'One of many such apartments in a block owned by a Kostakidas subsidiary company.' His eyes raked hers, hard and implacable. 'Shall I call my secretary and have her confirm that?'

Her eyes seemed locked with his, and she couldn't tear her gaze away. Slowly she shook her head. 'No,' she managed shakily.

She had little idea of the passage of time, and it could have been mere seconds, or several minutes, before she offered quietly, 'I arrived at the wrong conclusion.'

He moved close, and, placing a thumb and forefinger beneath her chin, he tilted it so that she had no option but to look at him. 'I have little doubt Shanna intended that you should.'

She felt nervous and unsure of his mood, and, unbidden, the tip of her tongue traced the curve of her lower lip.

'You were both an item,' she managed at last, and saw the faint glitter in his eyes.

'"Were" is the operative word.'

'Shanna doesn't appear to think so.'

'You believe I would maintain a mistress after marriage?'

'In normal circumstances ... no,' Leanne said honestly, and glimpsed his faint smile.

'Our relationship isn't normal?'

The sad part was that she had no knowledge as to whether he shared the overwhelming ecstasy she experienced in his arms.

'You find it difficult to condone the terms of our marriage?'

How did she answer that? With extreme caution, an inner voice prompted. Or, better, not at all. 'If we don't leave soon, we'll be late,' she reminded him, and his smile deepened, assuming a definite tinge of mockery.

'Evading the issue, Leanne?'

With a careless shrug she forced a faint smile. 'Perhaps,' she admitted, knowing that she didn't want to deal with it now. Maybe not ever. Although that was a fallacy, for eventually she would have no choice.

She looked at him carefully, seeing the strength in the depth of those dark, gleaming eyes, the sensuality apparent there, and wondered how she could possibly exist without him.

He lifted a hand to brush light fingers down the edge of her cheek, and her lips trembled as his head lowered to hers.

His mouth sought a possession that was flagrantly seductive, and any protest she might have made died beneath the mastery of his touch as he deepened the kiss. Of their own volition her hands lifted to link at his nape, her body arching towards his in silent invitation as she met and matched the depth of his passion.

His hands slid down her back to curve beneath her bottom, and she gave a soundless gasp as he lifted her up against him.

It seemed an age before he released her slowly down on to the floor, and his mouth gentled and became vaguely teasing as he tasted the lower fullness of her lip, then took it lightly into his mouth for a few heart-stopping seconds before trailing his lips up to brush against her temple.

'I suppose we *have* to attend the ballet?' Dimitri queried huskily, and she drew a deep, shaky breath.

'Krissie Van Hahme will be disappointed if we don't.'

'I could compensate for her disappointment with a sizeable donation.' He ventured, and smiled faintly as she shook her head. 'No?'

'The ballet was very close to Paige's heart. I think she attended every gala performance,' Leanne said wistfully.

'And you'd like to go.'

It was a statement she didn't deny, and without a word he caught hold of her hand and led her from the apartment down to the car, then he drove the short distance home.

Two hours later they were seated in the darkened auditorium viewing the opening scene of *The Nutcracker*. The music lilted beautifully, faultlessly crisp and clear due to superb acoustics, and Leanne was entranced by the excellent choreography, the beauty, colour and design of the scenery.

It was a magical evening, all the more special because of the way Leanne knew it would end. There was a sense of joyful anticipation as Dimitri threaded his fingers through her own and held fast her hand. Every now and again his thumb traced a soothing pattern back and forth over the softly pulsing veins at her wrist, and his smile was so incredibly warm it reached right down into the depths of her soul.

By tacit agreement they chose not to linger, refusing with polite regret Krissie's invitation to join a few select friends for coffee.

'Another time,' Dimitri promised, and the society doyenne gave Leanne a generous smile.

'I wouldn't want to waste a moment either, if I had this gorgeous man to go home with.'

He laughed, a deep, throaty sound that brought forth a wicked gleam in Krissie's eyes as she reached forward and placed an affectionate kiss on Leanne's cheek.

'Escape, darling. We'll catch up eventually.'

There was no need for words as the Jaguar negotiated the late evening traffic, and it seemed only a short space of time before the sleek vehicle slid to a halt outside the main entrance of the Toorak mansion.

Indoors they ascended the stairs, and on reaching their suite Leanne unpinned her hair, pushing her fingers through its length as she slid out of her shoes.

Dimitri was in the process of shedding his shirt, and she took a long look at him, glorying in the expanse of muscular flesh and the sheer animal grace that was his alone.

He lifted his head, almost as if he sensed her appraisal, and his eyes speared hers, dark and impossibly slumberous.

She stood transfixed as he moved towards her, and she trembled slightly as he drew her into his arms.

'It was a wonderful evening,' she said with sincerity, and his lips curved into a warm smile.

'It isn't over yet,' he promised gently as he lowered his head, and she almost cried at the depth of emotion apparent in him as his mouth closed over hers in a kiss that left her weak-kneed and totally malleable.

Her dress fell in a silken whisper to the carpet, followed by wispy underwear, then he drew her down on to the bed.

Their loving was long and incredibly gentle, becoming almost a sublimation of all the pleasurable senses as they sought to gift each other the ultimate in erotic satiation.

Afterwards they slept, tangled close together, and in the early dawn hours they made love again, then rose and showered before driving to Geelong for a picnic lunch.

It was late afternoon by the time they arrived home, and Leanne slid out from the car and turned towards him.

'Do you know what I feel like doing?'

'Should I ask?' Dimitri drawled musingly.

'What say we eat out tonight?'

One eyebrow slanted in mocking surprise. 'That's it?'

'Aren't you going to ask where?'

He moved round the front of the car and caught hold of her hand. 'OK. *Where*?'

She cast him an impish grin. 'A place I know,' she declared as they started walking towards the house. 'The chef's speciality is barbecued steak, a Greek salad, fresh bread, with fresh fruit and cheese to follow.'

'Should we ring ahead and book?' he queried, playing the game.

'They don't take reservations,' Leanne declared blithely as they gained the main entrance and entered the foyer.

'Let me guess,' he drawled indolently. 'You're planning a barbecue here on the terrace. Who gets to be chef?'

'You do. I organise the salad, the bread and the cheese.'

'Done,' he agreed, and his lips curved into a musing smile. 'Go and raid the kitchen while I check for any messages.'

Leanne inspected the large refrigerator and took out steaks, then extracted ingredients for the salad. She was in the throes of retrieving a bread-stick from the freezer when he entered the kitchen.

'Eloise called from the Gold Coast,' Dimitri revealed. 'She says it's urgent.'

Leanne closed the freezer door, then turned towards him, her forehead creased in a frown. 'Eloise works in the clinic. Why on earth would she contact me on a Sunday?'

'Perhaps you'd better ring and find out.'

Her eyes darkened, and her expression became faintly pensive. 'I'll have to check her home number in my address book.'

'I'll get things started here while you make the call,' Dimitri said, and with a murmured 'thanks' she moved quickly up to their suite.

Fifteen minutes later she returned to the kitchen to relay that the senior staff member she'd assigned to manage the clinic had been involved in a car accident and was in hospital. Another employee had been with her, and she too was injured.

'I have to go back,' Leanne declared, and caught his dark, probing glance.

'You can't delegate?'

She shook her head with regret. 'The clinic is without two operatives, one of whom manages the place for me. I'll need to screen suitable applicants, and choose someone as a replacement manageress.' She looked at him, pleading with him to understand. 'It's a good business, and I can't let it fall apart. I owe it to the staff, to the clientele.'

Something flared in his eyes, an infinitesimal flame that was quickly masked. 'How long do you envisage being away?'

'A week, at least. Maybe longer,' she offered with a slight shrug.

'You want me to arrange your flight?'

'Please,' Leanne said gratefully, chewing her lip as one thought after the other crowded her brain. 'My apartment is leased out, so I'll need accommodation.'

'Let's go into the study and take care of the details now. Then we'll eat.'

Leanne took the early morning flight to Coolangatta, caught a taxi to the hotel, organised for her car to be removed from storage, then took a taxi to the clinic.

The Gold Coast was a tropical paradise, famed for its beaches, coastal waterways, and the numerous luxury canal-front homes.

The air was fresh and clean, pollution-free, and she breathed deeply, aware of a sense of having missed the casual lifestyle and the slower pace compared to high-geared city living.

Monday was spent making phone calls, alerting employment agencies, and attempting to keep the clients happy. As promised, she put a call through to Dimitri on her return to the hotel, and after dinner she made contact with a few close friends. Then she showered and fell into bed to sleep until morning.

Tuesday was very much a repeat of the day before, except that it brought a dozen prospective employees, each of whom needed to be interviewed and assessed as to their qualifications, ability and appearance.

It should have been easy, but Leanne was aware how important it was for the staff already in her employ to get on with any new members. If anyone had a personality problem with a fellow employee it created tension that was often detected by the clientele.

To be scrupulously fair, she gave each suitable applicant a trial period and held meetings with the existing staff at the end of each day.

By the week's end she'd hired two operatives—one with an immediate start, the other due to commence on Thursday, and she was still undecided who to appoint as manageress. Colette would be ideal, although the only problem was that she wanted a managerial salary plus a small share of the profits.

'What do you think?' Leanne asked when she put a call through to Dimitri.'

'Why hesitate?' he countered. 'You say she's good. A share of the profits provides an incentive to keep the business running smoothly. Promote her, Leanne,' he drawled quietly. 'And come home.'

Home. It sounded *right*. It was certainly where she wanted to be, for although it was great to catch up with a few friends she didn't like returning to an empty hotel room at the end of the day, and she hated the long, lonely nights.

So she made the necessary call to Colette, had a contract drawn up, and took bookings for Friday and Saturday with some of her own personal clients.

On Sunday she rose early and walked down to the beach for a swim, then she ate breakfast in one of the many cafés lining the esplanade, returning to the hotel to shower and change before collecting her car and driving out to Sanctuary Cove to explore the many boutiques lining the harbour front.

It became a carefree day, and it was almost five when she reached the hotel and rode the lift to her appointed floor.

Feeling impossibly restless, she checked the room-service menu, picked up the phone and placed an order to be delivered at six, then she undressed and stepped beneath the shower, luxuriating in it far longer than was necessary as she shampooed and conditioned her hair.

There was no point in getting dressed, and she slipped into a towelling robe before switching on the television.

She had just finished her meal when there was a sharp, staccato knock at the door, and she dampened a slight feeling of apprehension as she crossed the room to open it.

CHAPTER ELEVEN

'DIMITRI!' Leanne's surprise was genuine, for he was the last person she expected to see.

Her eyes encompassed his rugged frame with a degree of hunger, then her lashes swept down to form a protective veil. More than anything she wanted to fly into his arms, to feel their warm strength enfold her close and give herself up to the magic he evoked the instant his mouth touched hers.

Yet she felt vaguely hesitant, afraid that if she allowed her feelings free rein she would be giving away too much.

'No welcoming kiss?' he prompted with indolent amusement, and she smiled, her eyes wide and guileless as she stepped forward.

'Of course. How are you?'

His eyes gleamed with latent mockery as his hands closed over her shoulders. 'Polite civility, Leanne?'

She wanted to cry out against his faintly taunting drawl, yet the words never left her throat, and she became filled with a familiar feeling of helplessness as he drew her into his arms.

Instinctively her face lifted towards his, her mouth soft and generous as he kissed her with such primitive hunger that it almost tore her fragile emotions to shreds.

Yet there was a sense of exultation in his tenuous control, and she flirted with the challenging thrust of his tongue, accepting his ravaging exploration before conducting one of her own.

It seemed an age before his mouth gentled, and she felt a slight shudder run through his powerful body as his hands slid down her back to rest possessively on the curve of her bottom.

His lips brushed hers, sensuous and stroking as he felt their quivering softness, and she heard his faint, husky groan as his mouth trailed down the sensitive curve of her neck to savour the madly beating pulse there before travelling lower, and he traced an evocative pattern down the deep V of her towelling wrap.

Her breasts burgeoned in expectation of his touch, and she made no protest as his fingers sought the tie at her waist, dispensed with it, then gently slid the wrap from her shoulders.

His eyes were dark and slumberous as he surveyed her delicate curves, and she swayed slightly when he lifted a hand and lightly traced the tender fullness of one breast before crossing to render a similar exploration to its twin.

'You're beautiful,' he said gently, letting his hand trail down to her waist, the indentation of her navel, before brushing low over her belly. 'So sweet and warm and giving,' he added huskily. 'I've missed you.'

The feeling was mutual, yet she couldn't bring herself to say the words. Instead, her hands shifted to his jacket and eased it from his shoulders, then she removed his tie. Her fingers slid to his shirt and she slipped the buttons free before tugging it off to join his jacket. Then she reached for his belt-buckle and unnotched it before freeing the zip fastening of his trousers.

He stood silent and still, and when she hesitated his hands covered hers, holding them fast.

'Don't stop.'

She looked at him carefully, her eyes wide and faintly luminous, unsure if she possessed quite the degree of courage to continue. A slight lump rose in her throat, and she swallowed it. 'Help me,' she begged quietly, unable to tear her eyes away from his.

A shivery sensation slithered the length of her spine as he lifted a hand and shaped her cheek, caressing it gently with his thumb.

'You've gone this far; why not continue?'

Of its own volition, the tip of her tongue edged out and ran a nervous path over her lower lip. His eyes flared at the movement, and she caught her breath, unable to release it for several long seconds as she became entrapped in the darkness of his gaze.

Slowly she sank to her knees on the carpet, and with extreme care she undid the laces of his hand-crafted shoes, and eased off one then the other before removing his socks.

Then she tugged free his trousers, and reached for the thin scrap of black silk shielding his manhood, her fingers slipping beneath the elasticised hem as she pulled the briefs slowly down over muscular thighs which flexed and tensed at her slightest touch.

There was a tremendous beauty in his arousal, a potent, virile force that was awesome when swollen to its fullest extent, and the desire to explore the delicate ridges was difficult to ignore.

Her touch was as soft and tentative as the brush of a butterfly's wing as she slowly traced the pad of her finger along a fold of skin, then trailed to the dark, springy hair nesting low at the junction of his powerful thighs.

With a sense of fascination she traced the outline of hair where it arrowed up the flat tautness of his stomach, then she lifted her other hand and gently completed the exploration before leaning forward to brush the lightest, briefest kiss to his shaft.

The desire to taste him, as he had frequently tasted her, gradually overrode her inhibitions, and he growled in husky approval as she followed her instincts, employing such incredible gentleness that he soon groaned out loud and reached for her, lifting her high so that she straddled his waist as he buried his head between her breasts.

Then it was her turn to cry out as he took one hardened peak into his mouth and rendered an erotic tasting until she begged him to stop.

'Put your arms round my neck,' he bade her as he shifted slightly, and she obeyed him, her eyes widening in startled surprise as he entered her with one sure thrust, his hands holding her hips steady as he began a slow, rotating movement that made her gasp at the degree of sensation he was able to evoke.

He kissed her, gently at first, then with such passionate demand that she was unaware of anything except the deep, sensual vortex into which she was being drawn.

At some stage she began to surface, and when she did it was to discover that she was lying on the bed, sated and drowsy in the aftermath of a loving that was unequalled by anything they'd previously shared.

It was all too easy to close her eyes and allow her attention to drift...to memories of Paige and Yanis, and the reason for her now unusual marriage.

Her love for the man who lay relaxed and sleeping by her side was both primeval and shameless. But did his emotional involvement go beyond the convenience of a willing partner in his bed? Worse, would he eventually tire of her?

Sleep had never been more elusive, and she eventually gave up counting each digital change of numbers on the bedside clock in the hope that it would aid escape from consciousness.

Moving quietly, she slid from the bed and padded barefoot to a distant window where the drapes gaped slightly and a slim stream of moonlight provided a soft, eerie light.

Carefully easing aside one long fall of heavy material, she cast her gaze out over the dark ocean whose smooth surface assumed a silvery gleam beneath the moon's glow.

The view was impressive, taking in the wide sweep of pale sand, the soft, curling waves with their gently foaming crests that looked so harmless tonight yet could swell into high-rolling waves that crashed dangerously into shore.

In a way it paralleled her feelings for Dimitri. Gentleness and sweet savagery. Possession that bordered on obsession.

There were lights lining the foreshore, a fairy tracery that curved seemingly out to sea as they followed the coastline all the way down to the northern tip of New South Wales.

Within the immediate periphery were bright splashes of neon, some constant, others flickering as they vied for the tourist dollar, and there was a steady river of headlights as traffic cruised the main arterial highways.

It was a scene she was familiar with, one she'd shared often from her apartment a mere kilometre distant.

She'd frequently assured Paige that she loved the Coast, enjoyed her independence, and valued her solitude. She'd lied, for her heart had been in Melbourne—with Dimitri. As it always would be.

Leanne heard a faint movement behind her, and she tensed slightly as hands curved round her waist and pulled her gently back against a warm, muscular frame.

'Unable to sleep?' Dimitri queried softly, and she felt his breath tease the length of her hair as he bent low to bury his mouth against the softly beating pulse at the edge of her neck.

She didn't trust herself to speak as a spiral of sensation unfurled deep within her and began to radiate through her body, activating every nerve-end, every cell until she was achingly alive.

'Dimitri——'

'Come back to bed,' he bade her gently, and she arched away from him as he nibbled the soft hollows at the base of her neck.

She groaned in silent despair, hating the way her body reacted to his dangerous foreplay. He had only to touch her, and she went up in flames.

His hands shifted to her shoulders as he turned her to face him, and she was powerless to evade his searching gaze as he tilted her chin.

His eyes were dark and languorous in the moonlight, his mouth a sensuous curve that descended
slowly to capture her own. She opened her mouth
to protest further, except that no words emerged as
he conducted a light, teasing tasting that was so
incredibly erotic it was all she could do not to
respond.

Her hands sought leverage against his chest as
she tore her mouth away, and she was powerless to
still the faint gasp as his hands urged her close in
against the force of his arousal.

'Don't——' Leanne begged. 'Please.' He stilled,
and she shivered slightly as one hand slid up to her
nape. 'We have to talk.'

It was hard to judge his mood, and she ploughed
on regardless, knowing that if she didn't continue
now she might never find the courage again.

'Our marriage,' she managed at last, each word
more painful than the last, 'was an arrangement we
were both thrust into, and I'm sure you wanted it
less than I did.'

He was so quiet that if his hands hadn't been
holding her captive she might almost have thought
he was some devilish figment of an over-active
imagination.

'I distinctly remember that marriage was my
suggestion,' he said in a deceptively soft voice. 'If
you remember, I was particularly insistent.'

'It's common knowledge why you did——' she
continued, but he intercepted silkily,

'Common knowledge to whom?'

Leanne was silent, recalling each and every one
of those damaging barbs and the pain they
had caused.

'You haven't answered my question,' he prompted quietly, and she effected a slight shrug.

'Naming names won't achieve anything.'

'Then tell me what was said,' he commanded softly, and she swallowed the sudden lump that had risen in her throat.

'You're a very astute man, Dimitri,' she allowed simply. 'I'm sure you can guess.'

He was silent for several seconds, his eyes dark and vaguely analytical as he viewed the visible signs of her distress. 'It would be advantageous to keep a considerable slice of Yanis's fortune "in the family"?' he queried with deceptive calm.

She replied with a trace of sadness, 'I've had it on good authority from several so-called friends that that was your main objective.'

His eyes hardened fractionally. 'Social acquaintances who obviously have nothing better to do than manufacture gossip and convey it by innuendo.'

'Perhaps.' She took a deep breath and expelled it slowly. 'Even so, there's some basis of fact in what they say, for if it hadn't been for Paige's illness you would never have considered marrying me.'

He looked at her carefully. 'You're certain of that?' he queried mildly, and she met his gaze unflinchingly.

'You could have any woman you want.'

'You find it inconceivable,' he ventured with deadly softness, 'that I might want *you*?'

She took another deep breath. 'I think we both have a right to happiness,' she said shakily.

'Are you unhappy?' he demanded softly—far too softly, for she saw evidence of his veiled anger in his eyes, and she shivered with the knowledge that she'd gone too far to retreat.

He reached out and switched on a wall-lamp in order to see her expression, and her eyes dilated at the invasion of light.

She closed her eyes against the sight of him, hating herself at that moment almost as much as she hated him. 'It's more than that.'

He was silent for a few long seconds, then he ventured silkily, 'Elaborate, Leanne.'

Dear God, this was far worse than her worst nightmare, for she wouldn't wake in the morning and know it was the magnification of a wicked subconscious.

'I don't think I can live with you any more,' she revealed quietly. There was nothing she could do to stop the slow ache of tears, or to prevent the well of moisture as they trickled slowly down each cheek.

'Because you love me?' Dimitri demanded gently.

She didn't possess the courage to utter so much as a single word. She wanted to dash away the tears, but she stood still, unable to move even if her life depended on it.

'Anything you feel for me is bound up in affectionate responsibility and a sense of loyalty to your father, to Paige,' she said shakily.

His hands moved to capture her face, and his eyes darkened measurably as he saw her tear-drenched cheeks and the sense of desolation evident in her expression.

'Does it feel like "affectionate responsibility" every time I make love to you?' He moved his thumbs and gently wiped away the moisture. 'Does it?' he demanded quietly.

It felt like heaven, and he had to bend low to catch her whispered negation.

'You and Paige,' he revealed quietly, 'brought so much warmth and love into my father's life, as well as to my own. I wanted to catch you close and never let you go.'

Her lips trembled. 'Yet you did.' It hurt so much to say it. 'I adored you.'

'You made me your hero,' Dimitri corrected her gently. 'Except heroes belong in fairy-tales, and you were a beautiful young girl who deserved to forge her own career and taste life before committing herself to one man. I intended to allow you a year, maybe two, of independence.' He smiled faintly, then brushed her temple with his lips. 'Except you froze me out, and became very clever at evading me, even going so far as to time your visits to Melbourne for when I was out of town. On the few occasions I managed to surprise you, you treated me with such polite civility it was all I could do not to shake some sense into you,' he concluded with dangerous softness, and she shivered slightly.

'Shanna,' Leanne ventured slowly, aware of the hidden pain deep within, 'seemed to consider——'

'I've never given her cause to believe she was anything other than——'

'A willing bedmate?'

'A pleasant companion,' he amended, and she pondered on the wisdom of pursuing the subject.

She looked at him carefully. 'I see.'

His hands shifted to her shoulders and he shook her gently. 'Do you?'

'I think so.'

'The day we married I pledged you my love and fidelity,' he reminded her quietly as he curved one arm down her back and brought her close.

'They were only words,' she declared shakily, hopelessly torn by a desire to believe him.

His head lowered and he fastened his mouth on hers in a kiss that was incredibly gentle at first, then became increasingly passionate until the mere melding of mouths was no longer enough.

Leanne gave a faint moan of assent as he slid an arm beneath her knees and carried her back to bed, where she gave herself up to the sheer delight of his lovemaking.

There was a piercing sweetness apparent, a joy that transcended the mere physical, and she clung to him unashamedly as he led her to the heights and beyond.

Afterwards she lay in his arms, content and at peace, her whispered words so low, they were little more than a soft caress. 'I love you.'

He trailed gentle fingers over her shoulder, the sensitive curve of her neck—a light tracing pattern that made her want to press her lips against his warm, vibrant skin. She heard the beat of his heart beneath her cheek, felt its strength as it powered lifeblood through his body. A beat that had pounded dramatically only a short while ago as he'd led her to a shattering climax mere seconds ahead of his own.

'You're my life,' he offered quietly. 'My dearest love. Never doubt it.'

The words whispered inside her head as she drifted into a dreamless sleep, from which she woke at the touch of a hand and the sensual brush of warm lips against her cheek.

'Mmm,' Leanne murmured, turning into his arms without any hesitation at all. 'Is it morning already?'

She heard his soft, husky laugh as he pulled her close. His mouth settled over hers in a long, drugging kiss that made her ache for more, and she gave a deep, pleasurable sigh as his lips trailed the pulsing cord at her neck and sought the valley between her breasts.

The sensual awakening was exquisite as her body surrendered to the mastery of his touch. Every nerve cell blossomed into renewed life, warm and beautifully responsive as he rendered tiny love-bites to the soft, swelling flesh beneath each breast.

The sensation drew from her a husky groan as he teased each pleasure spot to fever pitch, her body akin to a finely tuned instrument awaiting the maestro's stroke.

Her need for fulfilment was so intense that she began to plead with him, then beg as she raked her fingers down the length of his back, sinking her nails into taut, muscled buttocks as she urged him close.

Seconds later she gave a cry of relief as his fingers sought the moist crevice between her thighs, caressing the highly sensitised nub until its pulsing core drove her wild with a desire he didn't hesitate to appease.

A long time afterwards they rose and showered, then donned towelling robes when Room Service delivered their breakfast.

Leanne reached for the orange juice, then sank into a chair and began emptying packeted cereal into both plates.

'We have an hour before we leave for the airport,' Dimitri informed her musingly as he took the chair opposite.

Her hand paused in its action, and she cast him a stricken glance as a host of chaotic thoughts raced through her mind, the foremost of which was a series of appointments for the day ahead, plus a luncheon date with a few close friends.

'I can't,' she began, lifting a hand to tuck a stray tendril of hair back behind her ear. 'At least, not today,' she qualified, and saw his eyes narrow slightly. 'I promised Colette another day before she takes charge,' she hurried to explain. 'Besides, I owe it to the staff, the regular clientele. I can't just walk away before everything is satisfactorily organised.'

'I have a meeting scheduled in Melbourne for eleven,' Dimitri declared as he quartered an apple, then peeled and stoned a peach. 'One I can't postpone.'

'Dimitri——'

'Ring and let me know which flight you'll be on,' he said gently. With an economy of movement he reached for the steaming silver pot. 'Coffee?'

'Please,' Leanne murmured gratefully, taking the cup and saucer from his hand mere seconds later. 'Thanks.'

'For flying a few thousand kilometres to spend the night with you?' His eyes gleamed with humour, and she blinked at the degree of warmth evident in his gaze.

'The coffee,' she said with an impish smile.

'Hmm,' he mused as he reached out and stroked his fingers down her cheek. 'I should make you pay for that...' He trailed off suggestively, and a wicked grin curved her lips.

'You have a plane to catch, remember?'

With one fluid movement he got to his feet and moved indolently round to her side. 'Unfortunately.' He cupped her chin, then bent low and kissed her with such passionate intensity that she lost the ability to coalesce so much as a rational thought. Then he straightened, and directed a shattering smile at her. 'Don't be too long following me, hmm?'

She didn't trust herself to speak, and simply shook her head in silent acquiescence, watching as he turned and walked from the suite. Then she slid from the bed and made for the shower.

The day passed swiftly, and there was a spring to her step, a hidden depth to her smile that didn't go unnoticed by the two friends she shared lunch with in one of the newer hotels along the tourist strip.

'When are you going back to Melbourne?'

'Tomorrow,' Leanne informed them, and was greeted with two genuine and extremely voluble protests.

'We planned dinner at the Casino tonight, and Renée has tickets for a show tomorrow night. You *have* to stay. That gorgeous stepbrother of yours will never allow you to escape alone again. Oh, come on, Leanne,' Tricia pleaded. 'What's one more night?'

'I'll think about it,' she temporised. Which she did, qualifying her decision by rationalising that it wouldn't do Dimitri any harm to wait one more day. She'd waited *years*, and there was a certain degree of innate pride that forbade her from running back, no matter how much she needed to be with him.

So she attended dinner and the show, returning to her suite to sleep fitfully until she was woken by Room Service with her breakfast. Then she rang the airline, booked a late afternoon flight, and rang Eleni with the time of arrival.

The plane touched down and cruised along the runway before gliding to a halt in its allotted bay, and after disembarking she moved easily through to the arrival lounge.

'Leanne.'

Dimitri's achingly familiar drawl filled her with a treacherous weakness as she turned to face him.

There was a sense of *déjà vu*—same airline terminal, except that it was a different flight. However, this time there was no reserve or sense of uncertainty in her greeting. Only love, and a need to feel the warmth of his embrace.

Without hesitation she went into his arms and lifted her face as his mouth descended to take possession of hers in a kiss that almost blew her away.

'What took you so long?' he demanded huskily several minutes later.

She arched her head back and looked at him with such a degree of adoration that it made him catch his breath.

'I wanted to punish you a little,' she owned without hesitation, following the admission with a wickedly impish smile.

He laughed. A warm, deep, throaty chuckle that brought an answering gleam to her beautiful blue eyes. 'Indeed?'

She tilted her head a little to one side. 'I intend to make it up to you,' she promised solemnly, and he slanted her a long, musing look that sent her heart pounding against her ribs.

'Sounds interesting.'

'Oh, it will be,' she assured him. 'I had an hour on the plane to come up with several inventive possibilities.'

'I had planned to take you out to dinner,' he mocked gently.

Leanne reached up and kissed his chin, then she drew back and tucked her hand into the curve of his arm as they made their way towards the luggage carousel. 'Are you hungry?' she asked.

He reached forward and plucked her bag from the revolving belt, then led the way out to the car.

'For food? Or you?'

She slid into the passenger seat and fastened the seatbelt, waiting until he slipped in behind the wheel before venturing with teasing sweetness, 'A restaurant would be nice.'

He chose a small, intimate taverna specialising in Greek cuisine, and Leanne ordered her favoured dish of moussaka, while Dimitri settled for vine-leaf-wrapped meatballs and rice with a delicately flavoured sauce, and fresh, crusty bread. They drank fine wine, and savoured the meal, taking their time over coffee, then they walked arm in arm to the car and drove home.

Indoors they ascended the stairs to their suite, and once inside Dimitri extracted a long, slim envelope from the inside pocket of his jacket and silently handed it to her.

'For me?' Her puzzlement was genuine, and he smiled.

'Open it and see.'

Slowly she slit the seal, and removed two airline tickets...to Athens, departing the day after tomorrow.

'Dimitri——' Pleasure robbed her of words.

'A delayed honeymoon,' he relayed quietly, his arms closing round her slim frame as she reached for him. 'On a remote island in the Mediterranean. Far away from everyone.'

'Did I tell you how much I love you?' she whispered as his head lowered to hers.

'I'm hoping to hear you say it every day for the rest of my life.'

She smiled—a wonderful, achingly sweet smile that radiated from deep within her, lighting her eyes so that they resembled pure crystalline sapphire. 'I think I could manage that.' A faint laugh emerged from her throat as she tilted her head slightly. 'Of course, it's reciprocal, you understand?'

'Without question,' Dimitri answered solemnly an instant before he took possession of her mouth, and his erotic plunder made any further use of words totally superfluous.

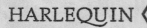 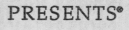

ANNOUNCING THE

FLYAWAY VACATION SWEEPSTAKES!

This month's destination:

Beautiful SAN FRANCISCO!

This month, as a special surprise, we're offering an exciting FREE VACATION!

Think how much fun it would be to visit San Francisco "on us"! You could ride cable cars, visit Chinatown, see the Golden Gate Bridge and dine in some of the finest restaurants in America!

The facing page contains two Entry Coupons (as does every book you received this shipment). Complete and return *all* the entry coupons; **the more times you enter, the better your chances of winning!**

Then keep your fingers crossed, because you'll find out by June 15, 1995 if you're the winner! If you are, here's what you'll get:

- Round-trip airfare for two to beautiful San Francisco!
- 4 days/3 nights at a first-class hotel!
- $500.00 pocket money for meals and sightseeing!

Remember: The more times you enter, the better your chances of winning!*

*NO PURCHASE OR OBLIGATION TO CONTINUE BEING A SUBSCRIBER NECESSARY TO ENTER. SEE REVERSE SIDE OR ANY ENTRY COUPON FOR ALTERNATIVE MEANS OF ENTRY.

VSF KAL

OFFICIAL RULES
FLYAWAY VACATION SWEEPSTAKES 3449
NO PURCHASE OR OBLIGATION NECESSARY

Three Harlequin Reader Service 1995 shipments will contain respectively, coupons for entry into three different prize drawings, one for a trip for two to San Francisco, another for a trip for two to Las Vegas and the third for a trip for two to Orlando, Florida. To enter any drawing using an Entry Coupon, simply complete and mail according to directions.

There is no obligation to continue using the Reader Service to enter and be eligible for any prize drawing. You may also enter any drawing by hand printing the words "Flyaway Vacation," your name and address on a 3"x5" card and the destination of the prize you wish that entry to be considered for (i.e., San Francisco trip, Las Vegas trip or Orlando trip). Send your 3"x5" entries via first-class mail (limit: one entry per envelope) to: Flyaway Vacation Sweepstakes 3449, c/o Prize Destination you wish that entry to be considered for, P.O. Box 1315, Buffalo, NY 14269-1315, USA or P.O. Box 610, Fort Erie, Ontario L2A 5X3, Canada.

To be eligible for the San Francisco trip, entries must be received by 5/30/95; for the Las Vegas trip, 7/30/95; and for the Orlando trip, 9/30/95.

Winners will be determined in random drawings conducted under the supervision of D.L. Blair, Inc., an independent judging organization whose decisions are final, from among all eligible entries received for that drawing. San Francisco trip prize includes round-trip airfare for two, 4-day/3-night weekend accommodations at a first-class hotel, and $500 in cash (trip must be taken between 7/30/95—7/30/96, approximate prize value—$3,500); Las Vegas trip includes round-trip airfare for two, 4-day/3-night weekend accommodations at a first-class hotel, and $500 in cash (trip must be taken between 9/30/95—9/30/96, approximate prize value—$3,500); Orlando trip includes round-trip airfare for two, 4-day/3-night weekend accommodations at a first-class hotel, and $500 in cash (trip must be taken between 11/30/95—11/30/96, approximate prize value—$3,500). All travelers must sign and return a Release of Liability prior to travel. Hotel accommodations and flights are subject to accommodation and schedule availability. Sweepstakes open to residents of the U.S. (except Puerto Rico) and Canada, 18 years of age or older. Employees and immediate family members of Harlequin Enterprises, Ltd., D.L. Blair, Inc., their affiliates, subsidiaries and all other agencies, entities and persons connected with this marketing or conduct of this sweepstakes are not eligible. Odds of winning a prize are dependent upon the number of eligible entries received for that drawing. Prize drawing and winner notification for each drawing will occur no later than 15 days after deadline for entry eligibility for that drawing. Limit: one prize to an individual, family or organization. All applicable laws and regulations apply. Sweepstakes offer void wherever prohibited by law. Any litigation within the province of Quebec respecting the conduct and awarding of the prizes in this sweepstakes must be submitted to the Regies des loteries et Courses du Quebec. In order to win a prize, residents of Canada will be required to correctly answer a time-limited arithmetical skill-testing question. Value of prizes are in U.S. currency.

Winners will be obligated to sign and return an Affidavit of Eligibility within 30 days of notification. In the event of noncompliance within this time period, prize may not be awarded. If any prize or prize notification is returned as undeliverable, that prize will not be awarded. By acceptance of a prize, winner consents to use of his/her name, photograph or other likeness for purposes of advertising, trade and promotion on behalf of Harlequin Enterprises, Ltd., without further compensation, unless prohibited by law.

For the names of prizewinners (available after 12/31/95), send a self-addressed, stamped envelope to: Flyaway Vacation Sweepstakes 3449 Winners, P.O. Box 4200, Blair, NE 68009.

RVC KAL